# Incidents

Barbara Winkes

*For D.*

# Chapter One

J ordan wasn't sure when it became a habit to end her regular morning walks at the coffee shop a few blocks down from their house. Maybe, because it was quiet, and she could focus on watching her baby sleep or make adorable noises, while Jordan enjoyed her decaf latte. Thoughts of the future were starting to intrude, given the fact that she was returning to work next week. Still, she was aware that she'd rarely been this much in the moment. Not for this long.

Being with Ellie, she had learned to enjoy herself and not feel guilty because there was always so much to do. The job had usually pulled her back into that mindset—the work never ended. There was always another case.

Jordan loved being a mother more than she had ever imagined, though she wasn't always calm about it. If people had felt entitled to give their opinion during her pregnancy, they hadn't stopped now that Meri was in the world. When she pushed her stroller along the sidewalk, it wasn't unusual that strangers came up to her and didn't keep as much distance as she would have liked. Jordan had always been protective of the ones she loved, and sometimes, staying polite became a real challenge—hence, her appreciation of a rather peaceful place to have a pretend coffee. To be honest, she barely tasted the difference anymore. She loved those mornings. They would soon be over.

She had seen her and Ellie's colleagues many times since she'd gone on maternity leave. She'd felt strangely detached from the subject when they mentioned cases. She'd never left the job, or any job, for that long. Not every single moment since her leave had been easy, and some moments she'd guiltily missed it. She looked forward to going back and being part of a group solving complex problems. She wanted to be home and play with Meri. Both couldn't happen at the same time.

Jordan studied the people around her, the student engrossed in something on his laptop screen. He was wearing earbuds. The barista cleaning the counter, looking like she was far away. She took another sip of her latte, her daughter's fingers curled around the index finger of her other hand. Bliss. She'd enjoy it while it lasted.

※

Pauline had come over for breakfast, happy to have more time than usual with her granddaughter. She sat with her in the living room while Ellie and Jordan had a last cup of coffee in the kitchen. Ellie, coffee cup in hand, was leaning against the counter. She followed Jordan's gaze, patting her back.

"Relax a little. They'll be fine, you know."

Jordan winced, aware of how transparent she was. She trusted her parents, and of course Ellie, but she could be territorial. No surprise there.

"Yes, I know."

"You're excited?"

"I don't know. It seems rude that people have to work instead of being with their babies."

Ellie sighed. "I know what you mean. But last week you basically solved Derek's case from home. You'll be happy to get right to it."

"Maybe. Will I see you today?"

In the past week, Ellie had been assigned to a task force that worked out of a different part of the building, investigating the death of an inmate in a nearby medium security facility. This had led to some unpredictable hours that didn't always match those of her other colleagues.

"Don't count on it. But I might be able to leave a little earlier today, make sure Pauline didn't teach Meri any swear words."

"I heard that," her mother-in-law commented.

"Sorry."

It had worked though. Jordan couldn't help smiling at the idea. No more stalling. All things considered, they were fortunate to be able to have their little family and thriving careers. She was grateful for all of it.

❦

A bit of irrational thought remained, because that was the cautious, jaded part of her, when she arrived at the station and took the elevator up to her floor. Colleagues had visited, brought gifts for the mothers and baby, and cooed over the latter. But they also had busy lives themselves, and what if they had simply moved on? Did she really still have a place in the elite unit she had worked so hard to be a part of?

The first thing Jordan noticed was that most desks were empty. Detectives were out on assignments, or they hadn't come in yet. She frowned. It was early for the place to be this deserted.

Her desk, which she had expected to be empty, was laden with files. All right—this was her welcome? Life had gone on without her, but since she was back, her colleagues expected her to do her part. Fair enough. Not even Lieutenant Carroll was in his office.

She sat down and opened the file on top of the pile.

"You're here, good. Come on, there's something I have to show you."

Derek Henderson had appeared out of nowhere.

"Hey." While she was happy to see a familiar face bringing some normalcy to this strange day, Jordan also wondered about the files being dumped unceremoniously on her desk. "You're going to fill me in on which of these are priority?"

"In a minute. I'd like you to meet someone."

"Relevant to the case?"

"Oh yes."

Still somewhat confused, she followed him across the room and along the hallway.

"Where is everybody? Is there something I should know?" she asked the moment Derek opened the door of the break room to her.

"We really missed you," he said. "And I think this answers all of your questions."

For a moment, Jordan stood, speechless, at the sight of her colleagues cheering. Ellie, who must have snuck away from the task force, closed the distance between them and hugged her tightly.

"Surprise," she whispered.

"It sure is a nice one."

On the table sat an impressive spread of pastries and donuts, fruit, coffee and juice. It was probably still okay to blame her blurry vision on hormones.

"Thank you," Jordan said. "I'm happy to be back." As much as she missed Meri already, that was the truth, too.

"Welcome back, Carpenter," the lieutenant greeted her. "You all take a moment, and then I want to see people at work. Henderson, I'd like those witness interviews on my desk this afternoon."

"Yes sir."

Carroll snagged a donut on a plate and a cup of coffee and went back to his office.

"I'm afraid I have to run too," Ellie said with regret. "I really didn't want to miss this."

"I'll see you later. Thank you." She and Jordan shared a quick kiss before Ellie left.

"We thought about champagne, but I think that wouldn't have gone over well with the boss," Maria Doss remarked. She stepped forward to embrace Jordan.

"Better days are coming. You must know Derek never brings coffee when you're not here, and Ellie's been with the task force, so everyone is seriously undercaffeinated."

Derek acknowledged the charge with a shake of his head.

"Some colleagues are more appreciative than others," he said, and Maria slapped his arm. "Yeah, that didn't help. I still like her better."

"I feel honored," Jordan said. "All those files on my desk though, they're real, aren't they?"

"Unfortunately." Maria sighed. "But don't worry, they're not all yours. In fact, a lot of them are my research for an older case."

"Nothing related to Shriver?"

Jordan wasn't sure why he sprang to mind, an ex-cop turned killer who had become infatuated with her. He'd disappeared the day she gave birth to Meri, and with so much on her and Ellie's minds, they'd rarely mentioned him at all. It was a silly question—they would have told her the moment there was any news. Still, on her first day back, she had to make sure.

"Nothing. Zip. Nada," Maria returned. "The fish must have eaten him by now. There's no way he could have survived that jump."

Jordan's stomach did a flip-flop at the graphic image.

"You say that because you think, or you know it?"

"Well, I wouldn't try, but we never found a body, and he hasn't resurfaced. Pardon the pun."

"All right. About those witness interviews Carroll mentioned," Jordan addressed Derek, admiring her strength as she put solely fruit on her plate. "What are we talking about?"

"Sad story," Casey Lyons commented. "Woman runs out of the house and straight into traffic. Driver couldn't stop in time and hit her. She made it to the hospital but died a few hours later."

Jordan winced. She hadn't stopped watching the news in the past few months, but all too often, looking at Meri made the rest of reality fall away, keeping the bad stuff on the periphery. She wanted a better world for her child and worked towards it. Thinking about the present realities of said world was daunting.

"So, there were witnesses? Her neighbors?"

"She didn't live in that building," Derek said. "We hope that our witnesses will be able to tell us what she was running from. I also want to stop by the doctor's."

"Let's go. I'll drive," Jordan informed him.

"I knew you were going to say that. I'll tell you more about it on the way. Oh, and Kate and I have a little something for you."

"You already gave us so much."

"Well, yeah, it's not for you. And it's only the beginning."

Jordan laughed. "Should I be scared? No, don't answer that. Thank you."

Kate and Derek, Meri's Godparents, had been visiting the most of all their friends. They insisted they didn't have plans of their own to start a family, though Jordan wasn't so sure. That was a subject for another day.

Before they left, Jordan put the gift bag from the children's store Derek handed her, into the backseat of her car.

Back to work. She was excited.

# Chapter Two

Ellie was happy and proud that the powers that be trusted her enough to be part of the task force, though her enthusiasm had at times given way to frustration.

A twenty-seven-year-old inmate in a women's prison was dead from an overdose. She and the other members of the team had been poring endlessly over witnesses' statements and visitor logs, only to come up empty-handed. No one had an idea how this particular brand of heroin had made it into Kayla Webber's cell, let alone how her body was only discovered when it was too late.

Early on, the sergeant heading the task force had decided that veteran cop Brigid Lofgren would go undercover to investigate the circumstances that had led to Webber's death. Ellie's task encompassed mostly research and paperwork. While it could be tedious at times, she understood that this was an important part in making sure Brigid would be as safe as possible once she was on the inside.

"Don't worry," she told Ellie when they'd taken a break away from the piles of documents. "You'll get it next time."

"Oh, I wasn't thinking about that." Ellie rarely missed an opportunity when she had the chance to advance her career, but her promotion to Homicide had also taught her to be realistic. Every single member of the task force was older than her. She wasn't a random choice either, but they still had years of experience on her, especially in undercover work.

"You should be. People know about your résumé, and the work you did with the FBI. It's no coincidence that you're here."

"Thanks...I guess?"

Brigid laughed. "Yes, that was a compliment, take it as such. But I get your point. You have a baby at home, and this is potentially going to be messy and dangerous."

"The more I hear about it, the more I'm fine with next time," Ellie admitted. "It's a mystery though. Inmates are tested, and they search visitors. How did the drugs get in?"

"We'll hopefully be the wiser after all of this."

Ellie thought of the reports she'd read, visitors caught trying to smuggle in all kinds of drugs and objects and getting caught. None of them had the kind of connections to obtain the heroin that had killed Webber.

They didn't have a suspect yet, but it seemed impossible for an inmate to pull this off on their own.

Brigid had only started to prepare for her role, and they were all aware that there was no margin for errors. Whoever was responsible for Webber's death was ruthless and smart, and they wouldn't appreciate anyone trying to unmask them.

For once, next time sounded amazing to Ellie, especially with Jordan barely back at work, and the two of them having to adjust once more.

❧

Both Jordan and Derek were silent when they pulled up on the curb of the apartment building from which Laura Mills had fled. It had rained over night, but Jordan almost expected to still see blood stains on the concrete. Instead, cars passed them by, and people walked on the sidewalk as if nothing had ever happened.

Something had happened to Mills, according to the doctor. Proof of sexual activity, no presence of semen. He had phrased it carefully, but even so they were coming to conclusions. People didn't jump up and desperately try to flee from consensual sex.

Her earlier excitement about being back at work vanished fast.

There were twenty-four apartments in the building.

"The donuts were a nice touch," she said, "though now I remember why I wanted to stay home with the baby."

"Remember that eventually, we always nail the son of a bitch."

It was cold comfort, chilling to think about. Laura Mills had gotten away only for a brief moment until she got hit by a car. The unsuspecting driver would forever carry that trauma with him. Sometimes it was hard to see a silver lining in the maybe.

They got out of the car only to realize that other cops were already doing what they'd set out to do.

"Ashley Carter, Major Crimes," the woman in the trench coat greeted them. "I'm sorry you if you weren't told yet, but this is now our case."

"Really? On what grounds?" Jordan was genuinely curious.

"On the grounds that we might have a serial predator on our hands," Carter answered. "Only this time, the victim didn't make it."

Jordan had restrained herself for some time, but given the context, she didn't make an effort to withhold the expletive.

"My thoughts exactly."

Though she found this an anti-climactic development on her first day, Jordan understood why Major Crimes thought this was a case more in their realm. Mills might as well have met a lover and tried to escape from something else, but this wasn't the best theory according to Occam's Razor.

"I'd like you to forward the statements you already took, if possible, today?"

"We'll get to it," Derek promised.

Jordan agreed. This was not the time to be territorial.

"Remember that pile on your desk?" he said when they were back in the car. "That part was not a prank. Damn. I can see their reasoning, but Carroll will not be amused about how the communication went on this one."

⊙≋≋⊙

"You're back already? Come see me in my office, Henderson?" Lieutenant Carroll asked as he passed them by in the hallway.

"That's right," Jordan mumbled, "I don't need to be a part of this."

"Lucky you. I'll be right back."

"You think?"

"Funny."

She chuckled and sat down to tackle the files still on her desk. It didn't take her long to make sense of them after having spent a substantial time on light duty before she'd gone on maternity leave. In some cases, there were follow-up phone calls to make. She had a fairly organized list before Derek returned, announcing, "I'm going to check if there are any of those donuts left. You want me to bring you one?"

"Sure, why not? Thanks."

Time went by quickly as they worked on how to make the best progress with the remaining files. Jordan closed the last one, looking up to realize she was in for a pleasant surprise.

"Hey. Look who came to visit Mommy at work." Meri stretched out her small arms, and Ellie handed her over to Jordan, who, for a few seconds, didn't care that they were in a police station. All was well with the world. Her curiosity won not much later.

"How come?"

"I had a bit of a slow day after all, so I decided to drive by home...Meri's all ready, fresh diaper and all. Should we risk it and eat at a restaurant?"

"*La Trattoria* has highchairs, and they are super friendly with kids," Casey Lyons who had joined them, suggested. "I also know another place called *SEVEN*?"

The bar run by Jordan's dad was friendly all right, but she didn't think she'd take Meri there just yet. Truth be told, she would be okay to end the evening with Ellie and Meri only. Everything and everyone else could wait.

"Not tonight," she said, "but thanks for the recommendation. I think *La Trattoria* is a good option. We leave now, it won't be too late."

"That's what I was hoping," Ellie chimed in. "I parked in the lot."

"We could take your car from here and you'll give me a ride tomorrow?" Jordan suggested. "Let me just go get Meri's gift. I left it in the backseat earlier. The Godparents have the best taste."

"Isn't she right about that?" Derek was pleased to hear the praise. "Hi, Meri. How's my favorite Goddaughter today?"

"I thought you only had one," Maria quipped.

One by one, their colleagues stopped by. Jordan determined that Ellie would be able to handle the situation and guard Meri's boundaries—or the boundaries Jordan had established when it came to anyone touching their baby. She left the room and headed for the elevator down to the parking garage to retrieve the stuffed animal, a powder blue cat, baby-safe and soft. Already, an army of stuffed animals was taking over more and more space in the nursery.

What a beautiful problem to have.

Walking towards the car, she held out the key and pressed to unlock the door. The shiny gift bag sat in the backseat, and she opened the door to reach inside.

Jordan was trained to sense minute changes in a situation, yet there was only a slight change of air that alerted her to the presence of another person, an inadequate warning for what followed. She reached for the door to steady herself, various thoughts running through her mind at once. Her gun. Jordan realized she had left it upstairs, only a split second before the blade sunk in again. The jolt of adrenaline still eclipsed the pain she should be feeling. Who? Her vision started graying out, but she was able to turn to get a look at her attacker, shocked to find she was a young woman with wild eyes, clutching the bloody knife. Jordan recognized her.

"You took my children. You took everything from me," the woman spat. "Now you pay." She charged again, though this time managed little more than a cut below her chest, as Jordan tried to wrestle the knife from her. Her knees buckled.

Joy Anne Deane spun around and ran. Struggling to breathe, Jordan tried to get her cell phone out of her pocket which seemed to take an eternity. Her vision faltered again, the concrete underneath her feeling like it was frozen. She was shaking all of a sudden as the blood soaked her shirt and pooled underneath her. She hit the last number called.

"Help...Joy Anne. She had a knife."

A dizzying mix of fear and failure was on her mind before pain and nausea drowned out everything else.

# Chapter Three

"Since you all don't want to spend time with us, I think I'm going to call my husband and ask him to order in," Casey declared. She was still rocking Meri and in no hurry to let her go. Amused, Ellie thought that Jordan would have an opinion on that if she were here this moment. Of course, she'd been home with Meri for most of the time, until today. Ellie was curious to see how her day had gone and also share Brigid's assessment.

"Another time. I promise."

"You better." Libby Marshall had briefly left the front desk to join the group. She was still wearing her headset. "I have to get back soon, but since Jordan isn't here yet, it's my turn. Come on, baby, come to Auntie Libby."

Ellie watched with pride. Meri already had a big extended family that loved her and watched over her. They were lucky to be surrounded by good people. She wondered if they should have dinner at the *SEVEN* after all. Meri was wide awake anyway.

"You all remember she's mine, right?" she joked as Derek picked up his ringing cell phone.

"We do, don't worry," Sam Potts assured her. "Congrats on the task force, by the way. That must be interesting."

"Thank you. It is, though I miss you guys already."

"Enjoy your time with the little one," Casey said. God knows they grow up so fast. Wow, listen to me—or better don't. Just enjoy."

"We will, thank you."

"Aren't you the cutest?" Libby gushed, holding Meri up high. She wrinkled her nose. "You definitely are, but I think a diaper change is in order."

"That's right, when it's time for that you're quick to give her back to Mommy," Ellie joked.

"That, and I think work is calling. No, Meri, I'm sorry, you can't play with this." Libby handed her back to Ellie before she could tug on the headset cable.

Derek was still on the phone.

"Sorry, what? It's a little loud here," Ellie heard him say. He walked a few steps away and then abruptly left. Ellie turned back to Casey, trying to ignore the sinking feeling in the pit of her stomach. She hoped this was something job-related, nothing to do with Kate. She hadn't spoken to her in a few days.

Ellie hoped Derek would return, so she could ask him about Kate, but minutes passed by, and it didn't happen. She'd send her a text to check in. And how long did it take Jordan to get that gift anyway? She had probably parked the car on the other end of the garage.

Meri was still the center of everyone's attention, so no one noticed that Carroll had left his office until he raised his voice.

"Harding!"

She spun around, the image of Derek rapidly leaving the room still on her mind. It didn't have to be related, did it? Carroll probably wanted an update on the task force.

"Come into my office, please."

Ellie checked her phone quickly, realizing that more time had passed than she thought since Jordan had left to get the toy.

She didn't like the tone of his voice, all of a sudden low and gentle, and the way everyone else had fallen silent. Even Meri looked quiet and concerned as if she understood something had changed.

"We can look after her for a moment," Casey reassured her. "You can see her from the window. As cute as she is, I'm not going to run away with her, I promise."

"Harding, now."

"Yes, sir."

She hoped this wouldn't take too long, so they could still have that quiet evening together with their little family after a quick diaper change for Meri. Ellie still clung to the hope that he might reprimand her for something, though she couldn't think of anything that might be on his mind. Was he going to take her off the task force?

"Please, close the door. Sit."

Ellie pulled the door closed behind her though she remained standing next to the chair, casting a quick glance at her friend holding her daughter.

"What is it?"

"There's no easy way to say this. Detective Carpenter was attacked with a knife in the parking garage. Henderson called from the ambulance."

The world came to a jarring halt. As if someone had dropped a giant weight on her, she stumbled, only vaguely aware of her supervisor keeping her up in a tight grip, his voice coming from far away.

"I know you need to make some arrangements now. Everyone's still here, let someone take your child home and drive you to the hospital."

Ellie blinked, the world around her a bizarre, nonsensical landscape until she realized tears were filling her eyes.

"How is she?" This was why Derek had left all of a sudden. She needed to hear that everything would be all right.

"We don't know much at this point. She lost a lot of blood, but she's alive."

While the last part came with a staggering relief, it also wasn't enough.

"You know she's a fighter. She's going to make it."

Ellie had never been so grateful for this man before.

"I need to go," she said, her voice shaky. She needed to be with Jordan, convince herself that she was going to be okay. Ellie wasn't sure she'd be able to walk or do any of the things she needed to do right now.

"I understand. I know that's the last thing on your mind right now, but I can give Sergeant Cameron a heads-up that you're going to need some personal time."

"Thanks."

She walked out the office as if in a fog, a part of her still hoping that this was a bad dream, and soon a crying baby would alert her that it was time for that diaper change. This couldn't be happening, not when everything in their lives was so perfect.

It was a tiny comfort when Ellie realized that she wouldn't need to explain anything to anyone. She couldn't have. Breathing took a lot of effort. She couldn't even figure out how they all knew already.

"I'm so sorry." Libby hugged Ellie close, tears in her eyes, too. Ellie disengaged herself quickly, knowing that her breaking point was close. She couldn't afford to think about herself.

"Ellie." Casey's voice was firm, a small measure of reassurance. "I know you want to go to the hospital, so why don't you let me get Meri home, and I'll wait there until someone else can take over?"

It was the sensible thing to do, but all Ellie could think about was Jordan advising her not to let anyone touch their baby, and she'd been only half joking when she said it. Would Meri think they'd abandoned her?

"I can drive to Jack and Pauline's too," Casey offered. "Whatever works best for you."

"No. Home. All her toys are there." Her voice sounded small and brittle, the way it had for months after her parents' death. But Jordan would make it. There was no other way. "Are you sure?"

"Yes, of course."

"Come with me." Sam Potts laid a hand on her back. "We'll go to the hospital. You can call Jordan's parents on the way."

"I'll let Kate know, if Derek hasn't already," Libby offered.

Ellie didn't object to anything but briefly wondered if she'd made a mistake by letting her friend, who had raised three children of her own, take her baby...or by being so naïve to think nothing bad could happen to them as long as they were happy.

Time became ungraspable.

On the way to the parking lot where Sam waited until she fastened her seatbelt in the squad car, Ellie barely noticed anything or anyone. At the same time, it was taking too long. Everything was taking too long. As soon as they were on the road, sirens blazing, she took her cell phone out of her purse.

"I can't do this," she said out loud. "I can't fucking do any of this." It didn't matter that she knew those particular fears were irrational. No one would blame her for anything. She needed to make that call, and then more. She needed to keep it together.

Sam didn't flinch at the expletive. She kept her eyes on the road.

"They're taking care of her. She'll be okay."

"How the hell do you know?"

"I don't," Sam said, matter-of-factly. "But I think the odds are in her favor. And I'm sure they want to know as soon as possible, because they'll do whatever it takes to help you."

Ellie didn't want to make things worse for anyone because she was scared out of her mind, but when Pauline answered, she could barely get the words out.

"Ellie, are you all right?" Pauline asked. "Is Meri?"

Ellie forced herself to breathe. In. Out. "Meri's fine. She...she's at home with a friend, Casey. I'm on my way to the hospital."

There was stark silence on the other hand, like the moment when Carroll had asked her to see him in his office. But this time, it was up to Ellie to deliver the devastating news.

"Jordan...She was attacked. We don't know much. I'm sorry. I'm so sorry."

"Oh, Ellie. How can we help?"

Taking a deep breath, Ellie answered, "I know that's a lot to ask, but could you go see Meri? I didn't know what to do. Jordan will be mad at me that I didn't go with her."

"Listen, Ellie. We'll head over to your house right now and make sure Casey has everything she needs first." Pauline was scared out of her mind, too, Ellie knew for a fact, but her voice was deceptively calm.

"Please, don't drive. Take a cab, or I could send someone..."

"It's going to be okay. I'll see you later. Jordan loves you, and Meri. That, more than anything, will see her through."

"I know." If everyone around her was trying to be optimistic, she couldn't crush their hopes, though what Ellie really wanted was to scream and not stop until she had certainty. "We're here. I'll let you know as soon as I learn anything."

Sam parked the vehicle, and together they headed for the entrance. The waiting area was already crowded with familiar faces, uniformed cops and detectives. Ellie headed straight for Derek Henderson, only to freeze at the sight of the blood on his shirt sleeves.

"She's in surgery," he said, pulling her into a hug. "We'll have to wait." He didn't say anything else, which she translated for herself. They couldn't let their guard down, not yet. In fact, there was nothing she could do until they got news from the doctor.

Except for one thing.

"Who did this?"

"She said, Joy Anne. Someone's looking at the footage from the garage now, and Maria is working on it. But unless we're all mistaken..."

"Joy Anne? Prophets of Better Days Joy Anne?" Ellie became aware that her voice had risen in a sharp angry crescendo. She remembered the woman. Joy Anne Deane had vilified a young girl in court, dismissing the abuse all of the women in the cult had been subjected to. Ellie and Jordan had started the process of adopting Ariel when family outside of the Prophets' abusive structures found her. They had tried their best to protect her and others. Joy Anne had called the women who testified, including Ariel, and the investigators, liars and traitors.

"She'll be held accountable. I promise you."

"What if it's too late for us? For Jordan?" The words tumbled out before she could stop them.

"Don't say that. Jordan will be okay."

Ellie had to believe him. After all he was the one who had seen her last. She tried to keep her imagination from running wild, but it was too late. A part of her was stunned that a woman had done this—then again, she had seen her share of women criminals lately, and in the case of the Deane family, they knew how women had been cruelly indoctrinated according to the leaders' ideology. She shook her head as if to clear the fog from her mind. Those theories didn't matter now. None of it mattered.

"Ellie! I was in class when Libby called. I came here as soon as I could."

She looked up to see Kate rushing towards her, to Ellie's surprise, Pauline with her. Ellie stiffened. The next person who put their arms around her would break her.

Pauline seemed to sense that because she laid a hand on Ellie's arm, briefly.

"Jack and Casey stayed at the house with Meri. They'll be here later. Do you need anything?"

Ellie needed good news, but it seemed petty to tell that to Jordan's mother who was just as afraid.

Kate exchanged a look with Sam, then she said to Derek, "Let's get some coffee quick," probably before the stains on his shirt registered with Pauline. Ellie would thank her later.

"Let's sit." Pauline gently steered her towards a row of seats. They had talked, here, not in the exact same seats, but this hospital, after Jordan had given birth. A day that had stayed in Ellie's mind as both frightening and joyful. Fear was the only thing left. She raised her eyes at Pauline, desperate to make her understand what she couldn't say out loud.

"I know you're afraid. I am too. We've all been through a lot of bad things, and we'll get through this too. Soon you'll be back home with Meri."

What if she was wrong? What if they were all wrong? The urge to scream hadn't abated yet. She wanted to be with her daughter, and the woman she loved. Instead, Ellie was stuck in this room having to answer politely to the never-ending stream of colleagues who expressed their support, because all of them knew, everything could change in a heartbeat.

Every one of them probably knew someone who had gone to work expecting to come home at the end of their shift when they didn't. When Kate carefully put a cup of coffee into her hands, Ellie thought of the day they'd lost Jensen Baker, Kate's fiancé at the time. The cold grip of fear threatened to choke her once more.

Joy Anne Deane and her clan thought that she deserved to go to Hell. If that was her intention, she had succeeded, because that's exactly where Ellie felt she was.

Distantly, she noticed that Derek had changed his shirt.

The waiting continued.

# Chapter Four

K ate and Derek had gone to spend the night with Meri so both Jack and Pauline could be in the waiting room. Ellie still managed to sit straight up though she wasn't sure she'd be able to do anything else, if asked. Her thoughts were going around in circles, on occasion settling on the last bits of conversation she'd had with Jordan. In the morning, she'd joked about her sudden reluctance to go back to work. Why? Why had she spent hours on that task force missing time with her family, when a catastrophe was around the corner? Shouldn't she have known?

A suspicious quiet settled over the room. Ellie jumped to her feet when she saw the man in scrubs walking towards them.

"You're all here for Detective Carpenter?" He didn't look like someone about to deliver the worst of news, did he? Would it show in his face, his tone?

"I'm her wife. How is she?"

"She's stable," he said, and for the first time since Carroll had informed her about the attack, Ellie was able to take a deep breath. She barely noticed that some of the latest coffee someone had brought her had sloshed over her hand.

"She's lost a lot of blood, and the next forty-eight hours will be critical." If she'd wanted to hug him before, Ellie was battling the mild impulse to slap him for that TV doctor response. She'd never thought that she'd ever be in the position to hear it from a real surgeon. "We are optimistic," he added. "We could provide timely intervention, and your wife is in good health. Dr. Yang will let you know when you can see her and explain things further."

"Thank you." It sounded like a whisper to her, but his tired smile told her he'd heard her.

Jack handed her a couple of paper tissues, and she finally wiped her hand. Back to waiting.

"I should call Kathryn," she said. Even saying those words seemed to cost a lot of energy. She wasn't sure how she'd handle that call, or how Kathryn would.

"We'll take care of that," Jack promised her, and all she mustered was a tired nod.

Ellie did make a call to Kate, though, to check on Meri, and update Kate and Derek on Jordan's condition.

"That's good news." Kate sounded tired, too, but relieved. "It's all good on our side. She's fed, bathed and right now, sleeping."

"I'm so sorry."

What Ellie really meant was that she was terrified and feeling guilty towards Meri, but she couldn't voice her complicated emotions.

"Don't be. We signed up for this, remember? Not just the fun times. Take as much time as you need."

"Thank you. The doctor is here now. I've got to go."

Ellie got up once more, took a couple of steps and hesitated.

"Go," Pauline said. She didn't need any more prompting.

As Ellie stepped into the room, she was going through the moments they had spent together in the past twenty-four hours or so, falling asleep next to each other, getting up early to get Meri ready for her day with Pauline, making breakfast.

That damn case wasn't even a current one. The founders and many other members had stood trial and were serving prison sentences. Joy Anne Deane had been given a chance to live her life free from the women-hating murdering cult she was born into—she had made a choice all right. Pushing the anger aside, Ellie pulled the chair closer to the bed, sat down and took Jordan's hand.

*I can't do any of this without you.* "You scared me." As soon as she'd said those words, she regretted them. "I love you." That was better. "I promise you won't have to worry about anything. Just rest and get better." At first sight, it was impossible to tell the ordeal she'd been through. Jordan looked still and relaxed in her medicated sleep, but Ellie wasn't fooled. A closer look revealed specks of blood on her hand, small cuts. *Defensive wounds?*

She tried to relax her own fingers, realizing she'd been gripping the hand in hers like a lifeline. Her heart was pounding from too much caffeine as much as the images haunting her. She hadn't even been at the scene yet, and Meri probably still hadn't received her gift, or maybe Derek had taken it home.

"Meri is safe at home with Kate and Derek," she whispered. "Everyone wants to help. We got this. I know we do."

The waiting game had only just begun. Ellie couldn't imagine what it would take to remove her from this space. She was incredibly grateful for their friends and family who had sprung into action. And so, so tired.

❧

Against all odds, she must have nodded off, jolting awake when someone touched her shoulder. It wasn't anyone from the medical staff, but Detective Maria Doss. Ellie tried to interpret her expression, not coming up with anything. Nothing she had to tell her was any priority to Ellie at the moment. She knew there was a case to make, someone to hold responsible, but those thoughts weren't more than flashes. She'd deal with them later.

"I'm sorry to disturb you, but could I talk to you outside for a moment?"

Ellie was disturbed all right. The doctor had filled them in before she was allowed in the room. Two shallow stab wounds, and a third one that had given them more concern, potential complications to watch out for even after they'd repaired the damage. Ellie was disturbed, and so were Jack and Pauline. They had taken a moment with their daughter before Ellie returned and fell asleep in this chair.

"Ellie?"

"Sure. I'm coming."

Once outside the room, Maria didn't waste any time. "We picked her up earlier, near the house of the people who foster her children. She still had the knife on her."

"That should be an easy case to make." Ellie was fairly surprised at how calm her voice sounded.

"Yeah," Maria agreed. "She's just digging herself deeper, keeps talking about how it was justified to fight back, because the system took her children."

"She would have married them off to some old guys in the cult once they got out of prison?" That was meant to be sarcastic, but to Ellie's horror, Maria didn't deny the charge.

"Perhaps, maybe even sooner. It looks like she was reaching out to a couple of family members who tried get the Prophets back up and running, child marriages included. Of course, hers are still young."

She wanted to throw up. "I thought they were all locked up. And her children are what, pre-school?"

"Some brothers and cousins thought their time had come. Some of it might be fantasy, but either way those children were not safe. Not to mention her homophobia and overall being a horrible human being."

Ellie would be the last to disagree. When they worked the case, she thought it was important to consider the role trauma played in the women's cooperation with harrowing practices. But Ariel's birthmother had seen it for what it was and worked to get Ariel and herself out.

Ariel would be heartbroken, and it was possible she already heard the news. At least she had a loving family that would protect her. Ellie would still have to talk to her. She would want to come visit.

"Anyway," Maria concluded, "She'll be with us for a bit. The FBI will want to talk to her, since it was their case too."

"Torres is coming?"

"I don't know yet. I just wanted to tell you where we are. There's no way she's getting out of this."

"I appreciate it. Thank you." She was about to go back in when she saw Jack wave to her. Kathryn was with him, and a moment later, Ellie found herself wrapped in another tight hug. "Everything will be fine. She'll be fine, right? If you ever need help with the baby, please, let me know. I can come over and take care of her."

"We'll see. Thank you. You can go in for a moment. I have to go to the bathroom," Ellie said, not wanting to start an argument. She wasn't sure how Jordan felt about Kathryn babysitting, because she had never mentioned it. Having her over, visit her with Meri, they had done that, but this was a different conversation altogether. There was another call, unavoidable, but that didn't mean she dreaded it any less.

Ellie walked to the restroom a few feet down the hallway, went inside and locked herself in a stall where she gave herself time to cry. She didn't have long, or someone would come after her. She simply stood, leaning against the wall, letting the tears fall. This was all the time she was going to get. She needed to step up now. As a mother, a spouse, and a cop. After she washed her face at the sink, the woman staring back at her from the mirror reflected steel resolve. This was what she needed to project, no matter how brittle she felt inside.

Ellie went back to Jordan's room, largely ignoring everyone else for the time being. She'd make that other call early in the morning.

# Chapter Five

I t felt like she was swimming through molasses dark and suffocating, struggling to reach the surface. Jordan remembered that feeling from a time or two before, escaping from a drugged state to something resembling consciousness. She'd faced shocked adults one time, as a child, when one of her biological parents' guests amused himself getting her high.

She'd come face to face with a twisted predator another time, many years later.

In the present, her mind was muddled with a mix of memory and vague sensations. The soft voice coaxing her to the present didn't present any danger. It belonged to Ellie.

"It's okay. Take your time."

"What she said."

That voice was unfamiliar, but equally unthreatening. Her vision started out as a dizzying blur of colors and shapes as she struggled to focus.

A hospital. Ellie, and a man in a white coat. She couldn't come up with anything else, the realization causing instant panic. Did she have an accident? Had Meri been in the car? The last thing she remembered was her colleagues fawning over her at the station. She desperately tried to form the words, but it wouldn't come out.

"Meri is fine," Ellie whispered. "She wasn't with you." She had to lean very close, enough for Jordan to realize she looked pale and exhausted. It made her sad. She seemed to have little control over her own expression, because something changed in Ellie's.

"What is it?"

"So...tired," she managed. *You seem to be too. What happened?* Most of that string of words only happened in her mind, but now that there was no immediate danger to Ellie or Meri, she could rest a little while longer.

The next time she came to, she was still tired, though a bit more alert and able to communicate.

"What happened?" It was still chaos on her brain, the station, something about a gift Derek had brought...pain.

The question seemed to startle Ellie, as if she wasn't sure it was the right moment to tell.

"Everyone is...safe?"

"Yes, of course. Dr. Yang is on her way. She wants to examine you. I think we should let her do that first."

"Oh crap," she cursed weakly, not as a reaction to Ellie's words, but to the image that was forming. "She had a knife."

"You remember?"

"Some...of it."

She was still on enough medication to mask any pain, but everything that came to mind made her cringe hard.

"I think I do. The woman from the cult. Joy Anne."

"Yes. Maria was here earlier. She's in custody. Oh, and here's Dr. Yang."

"I'm glad to see you with us," Dr. Yang said with a bright smile. "Mrs. Carpenter, if you could step outside for a moment?"

Ellie didn't correct her, just leaned down to kiss Jordan's temple. "I'll be right back," she whispered.

All of a sudden, Jordan wished she wouldn't leave. Her grip on reality still felt too fragile.

Outside the room, Ellie assumed Dr. Yang would give Jordan the same information as she'd received earlier. They were extremely lucky. The "millimeters would have made a difference" kind of lucky. She shuddered. As long as she was in the room, especially now that Jordan was more lucid, she could make herself believe everything would be okay. A few feet away, and her mind went into overdrive.

Kate had to go to work and classes, and Derek had a job to do as well. Jack and Pauline wanted to be with Jordan too. Ellie wasn't yet ready to consider Kathryn in that equation, and she wasn't going to raise the question with Jordan before she was back on her feet. Carroll had told her to take her time, but how much time? Dr. Yang hadn't yet mentioned anything about when Jordan would be able to go home.

She longed to hold Meri. Ellie was sure that Jordan did too.

She needed all the support she could get, though Ellie wasn't ready to go back to the waiting room where she'd have to talk, reassure others. Not yet.

**

"Hey, partner."

The next afternoon, Derek came by to update both of them and, Jordan assumed, also take her statement. That gave her the opportunity to convince Ellie to go home for a little while, spend some time with Meri and to have some food, shower, and a few hours of sleep. Jordan knew that Ellie likely wouldn't follow her advice on the latter. Jordan couldn't blame her as she, too, found herself with some separation anxiety.

"You gave us quite the scare."

"Not on purpose."

"I know. How are you feeling?"

"Like I was hit by a truck?" she suggested and flinched. The day they met the Major Crimes detectives at the scene, came to mind. "Maybe not...such a good metaphor."

"I hear you." He seemed to hesitate.

Jordan struggled to reconcile the present moment with her spotty memory of the attack, and afterwards. "You were there." She knew what it meant, too. "Thank you." Dr. Yang had informed her that with the blood loss, minutes would have made a difference. What a mess. Her saving grace, besides her partner acting quickly, was that Joy Anne might have harbored a lot of hate, but she wasn't that strong. Two shallow stab wounds. One...not shallow.

"You managed to call. You did the hard part." Nevertheless, his expression was haunted.

"I don't know. The hard part will be when all those good meds wear off. I'm still pretty loopy."

"You're doing great."

"Great enough for a statement?"

"We can do this another time. That woman isn't going anywhere."

"She surprised me." Jordan felt her face heat, from the medication maybe, or something more sinister like shame. She had always thought she'd make her way back to work seamlessly, as if she'd never left, but had she been distracted? Lost her instinct?

"Oh no, come on, that was not your fault. She planned this, and we're going to prove it. It wasn't like you could expect any danger in that particular moment."

Reality hit her. She wasn't going to go home tomorrow, or the day after, which meant it would take even longer until she'd be able to work again. Not that she could even leave this bed at the moment.

"I'm really sorry," Derek said. "We have the footage from the parking garage, and she was falling over her feet to confess. She's going away for a long time."

That was somewhat of a relief, though it wouldn't make much of a difference to her life in the near future.

"Could you just leave me alone for a moment?"

"Is everything all right? The doctor was happy with your progress so far, right?" he asked, alarmed. "Ellie said—"

"Please."

She didn't wait for him to leave, just turned her head a fraction and let the tears fall.

# Chapter Six

E llie didn't sleep.

After she arrived at the house, she went straight to the living room, where Pauline sat on the couch with Meri, and took her daughter into her arms.

"Derek is with her now," she said. "She's been awake more." She didn't know whether to laugh or cry when it looked like Meri was wrinkling her nose.

"That's good," Pauline said softly. "We are fine here. Kate is going to come by after her class. Why don't you take a shower and lie down a bit, and I'll make us something to eat?"

"I could eat," Ellie admitted. "And even Meri thinks Mommy needs a shower, so I'll do that first."

"Of course."

"I think I'll need to stop by the station too, to let the boss know where we're at. I'm already on loan for the task force, and Jordan has been out for some time."

"She's not going to like being out for longer."

There was no question. Ellie handed Meri back to Pauline.

"I won't be long," she said before heading upstairs.

The shower and a change of clothes made her feel a bit more like herself. Ellie still didn't want to take too much time to think or look at her tired self in the mirror. She could always doze for a few hours at the hospital.

Ellie came down to find Pauline had an early dinner on the table. Her growling stomach took notice.

"It's from the bar," Pauline explained. "Jack brought this by earlier."

Taking a first bite, Ellie could barely hold back an inappropriate sound. "This is so good. Thank you so much, for everything."

"That's the least we can do. I hope you don't mind that I put a few containers in the freezer. You'll have a few quick meals when you need them."

"Again, thank you. This helps a lot."

A short time ago, Ellie wasn't even sure she'd feel like having food, but she had to be realistic. She'd need to keep this schedule for some time to come, and she couldn't let Jordan down. Or anyone else.

She didn't even realize she was tapping her foot on the floor until Pauline spoke to her gently. "Ellie. You can allow yourself to be here for a moment."

"I know," she said with a sigh. "Derek will stay for a bit. He'd let me know right away if anything changes."

"I know you want to be with her 24/7. No one understands that more than I do, but you need to take care of yourself too. She'll need your help."

For some time to come, Pauline hadn't said it out loud, but Ellie heard the words anyway. She blinked away fresh tears.

"I get that."

"So have coffee and dessert with me, and then you can head back."

Ellie wasn't sure her body could handle any more caffeine, but the prospect of it, combined with something sweet, wasn't something she could refuse. She couldn't let herself be lured into too much comfort. Derek had a necessary job to do. She could take a few more minutes. Everyone was doing their part.

They talked a little longer over coffee and a piece of the cheesecake that Jordan had frequently craved while pregnant. On a whim, she packed a piece to bring to her.

She kissed Meri and hugged Pauline, then went back on her way.

Ellie was going to make it quick, have a word with the lieutenant, and then head back to the hospital. However, Carroll wasn't in his office. Instead, her friend Libby found her. Ellie told her what she could, resisting the urge to fidget.

"She's here again. This time, the FBI wants a piece of her."

It took Ellie a few seconds to realize who Libby was talking about.

"Where?" She sounded calm and reasonable to her ears, though she didn't miss the alarm in Libby's expression.

"I shouldn't have said that. They're busy with her. You're going to the hospital, right? I wanted to come by after my shift."

"Come on, I work here. I'm going to find out either way. I just want to take a look at her."

"What good would that do? A.D.A. Esposito has been here all day. She's got this."

"I don't doubt that. Now don't keep me away from my wife any longer."

Libby still looked doubtful but relented. "They're probably still in there."

"Like I said. I just want to take a look."

Ellie meant what she'd said up until the moment she knocked on the door and realized that Joy Anne Deane was alone, save for the officer guarding her. Wes Martin. They'd gone to the academy together and stayed friends afterwards. Ellie cast one look at Joy Anne Deane staring back at her smugly.

Did she recognize her? Ellie who had been involved in the operations that brought down the Prophets of Better Days, had taken statements from some of the women, though not her. She might recognize Ellie from the trial.

"Wes, could you do me a favor? Leave us alone for a second?"

"I didn't know you were back at work already. Jordan is doing okay?"

He all but whispered the second part, Joy Anne craning her neck curiously.

"I just need to ask Ms. Deane a question."

Deane bristled. Ellie could guess why—all the women in the cult were "Mrs.," real marriage certificates or not.

"I'll be outside," Wes said.

Ellie waited until he'd closed the door, then she took a seat in the chair across from the woman and studied her.

"Now what? I know you. You're not supposed to be in here, but even if you were, none of this is of any worth to you without my lawyer present."

"That's not why I'm here. You were caught on camera." Ellie's stomach churned at the thought of those images. "That's done. I wanted to be the one to tell you that you failed, whatever it was you were trying to achieve. My wife survived, and you? You'll never get the chance to harm your children again. I'm a mother too, and I have to tell you I'm happy with this outcome."

Wes would return any minute, and so would the FBI agents present. Ellie was aware that every moment in the room with Joy Anne Deane was draining her. She'd never be able to reach her—Joy Anne was all stubborn prejudice, poisoned by the ideology the founding brothers had forced on her. It was tragic, horrible—but only one person was responsible for the choices she had made afterwards.

"This, you are unnatural, and so is the woman you call your wife." Joy Anne Deane nearly spat the words. "It's a mockery of family and marriage, and you broke ours apart because you couldn't have the real thing."

Ellie was on her feet before she knew it, feeling the blood drain from her face at the grotesque accusation.

"I pity you, Ms. Deane," she said. "You are jealous, and I'm starting to understand why. You don't understand love because you never had it."

Ellie's jaw dropped when Joy Anne spit at her for real. She'd barely gotten out of the way in time when the door opened.

"All right, break's over."

In a heartbeat, the foolishness of her actions registered with Ellie.

"Ellie, hi. Let's step outside?"

Wishing she had punched Deane, but aware of how much additional trouble that would get her into, Ellie had no choice but to follow Dr. Bethany Roberts out of the room.

"Oh God, I'm really sorry. I didn't mean to...I wanted to call."

Much to her surprise, Bethany drew her into an embrace. Ellie let her for a few seconds, before all that steel resolve would have given way to a meltdown, this time not in private.

"That's okay. As soon as I heard I took the next plane. This was my case too," Bethany added quickly. "I wanted to stop by later, if that's okay?"

"Of course. Jordan will be happy to see you."

"It's kind of you to say that. Unfortunately, I can't ignore what you just did..." She sighed. "But I can work around it. The evidence is damning, so you couldn't do much harm. The first part was almost legit."

"Thanks...I guess."

Bethany laid a hand on her shoulder. "I'll see you later. Give Jordan my best, okay?"

"I will."

"How is she really doing?"

"She'll be okay. You'll see."

Without having achieved her real objective, Ellie went back to her car. How was it possible that her life had come to feel this unreal? Maybe she was still in that bizarre nightmare.

Jordan was sleeping when she returned, which gave her a moment to get some coffee—by now, she needed it. Before she could pass on Bethany's well wishes and news about her imminent visit, she'd have to confess how she'd run into her in the first place.

There was something she couldn't put off any longer.

Becca Crane, Ariel's aunt who had taken her in, answered the phone.

"Ellie, I thought we might hear from you. How are you both doing?"

"Better, thank you. Could I speak to Ariel?"

Ellie wasn't sure if she sensed hesitation on Becca's side. She could imagine this wasn't easy for Ariel either, but she'd prefer to be kept up to date, Ellie was sure.

"I'll get her. They said in the news they arrested someone from the cult?"

"Yes."

She heard distant voices, then Ariel came on the phone.

"This is horrible. I'm so sorry."

"Thank you, Ariel. I just wanted to tell you Jordan is doing better. Would you like to come by this week? If you give it a couple of days, she'll be up for more visitors."

"Why would she want to see me?"

She could hear tears in Ariel's voice. Ellie realized that this call wouldn't be quick, or easy.

"Why would you doubt that? Of course she wants to see all our friends."

"But it's because of people like me that she got hurt."

She'd been afraid Ariel would go there. It was the reason Ellie had stalled, hoping that the more time passed, the more Becca would be able to deal with all of Ariel's irrational notions.

"That is so not true. She got hurt because of one person. Joy Anne is the one to blame, not you, or anyone who managed to get out and build a new life."

Ariel wasn't convinced. "Joy Anne knew that you were trying to adopt me. She thought I was a traitor, and that you influenced me. I would understand. I hate myself."

"Ariel, stop!" Realizing that this tone of voice wasn't helpful, in their conversation or énever hate you. Joy Anne called a lot of people traitors, and she was wrong. She is wrong." The memory of Joy Anne's hateful tirade made her shudder. "Please, don't believe anything else. Jordan will tell you the same, I promise you. Are we okay?"

"Yes, sorry. I mean yes."

Ellie would check up on her, but for now, she felt this was all she could do.

As she ended the call, she realized Wes Martin had left her a message.

*You should give the Lieutenant a quick call.*

It couldn't be worse than talking to an inconsolable teenager who felt like she should carry the weight of the world on her shoulders. With Jordan still asleep, Ellie seized the opportunity hoping Carroll wouldn't have a lot of time.

"Sir, before you say anything," she started after she answered. "I apologize. It won't happen again."

"You're damn right it won't," he grumbled. "I think you're aware you just gave the defense attorney a gift?"

"I didn't threaten her. She spit at me!"

"Yes, and she was still right in one thing. You shouldn't have been in the room." He sighed. "I suppose it could have been worse, but you stay away from now on, you hear me?"

"Loud and clear, sir."

"Good. Everything else going well?"

"Yes. We were lucky." She wondered when she'd be able to say that without her eyes welling up.

"Thank God," he said. "Before you go, Cameron asked me to pass on news regarding the task force. There's been another suspicious death in the facility."

"Oh no."

"I know it's a difficult situation for you, but they're asking when you might be able to come back, at least part time."

She was seeing stars from a lack of sleep.

"Honestly, I don't know. I think Jordan might be able to come home next week, and we'll take it from there. Thank you for the heads-up though. I'll give them a call."

"You're welcome. And IA might want to drop by for a brief chat, though I think Dr. Roberts softened them up already."

"Really?" Knowing that she didn't have a lot of room to argue, Ellie relented. "I'll talk to them too. They'll know where to find me."

"You give Carpenter my best wishes. And remember to eat and sleep."

"Yes, sir," she said before ending the call. Ellie was almost surprised at the smile forming on her face. She knew that a lot of people in their lives cared. It was nice to be reminded.

# Chapter Seven

E llie was overjoyed to find Jordan was starting to get fidgety, talking about when she'd be able to go home—even if they both knew, for the moment, it was just talk. She was still groggy, though moments of discomfort and outright pain were starting to pierce through the cocoon of medication.

"It's not so bad," she insisted. "All progress, right? I hope you're getting some sleep too? Though, and I say this with love, you don't look like it."

Ellie couldn't help it, she laughed.

"That's funny?"

"I can catch up on all the sleep in the world once you're home. I don't want to be anywhere else." She had decided she'd break the various news gently, one subject or two at a time. "I talked to Ariel earlier. She'll come by in a couple of days."

Jordan's expression told her that she had a good idea of how that conversation had gone.

"I reassured her in every way I could. The Cranes love and support her. I think that's all we can do."

"There's more."

"There is. I stopped by the station before I came here and ran into Bethany earlier. She also wanted to visit...and we hugged. I guess that means I'm now friends with the ex?"

Jordan obviously found this amusing, though she turned pale the next moment.

"Crap, this hurts. Don't make me laugh just yet."

"I'm sorry. I'll remember that." Ellie leaned close to kiss her softly.

"Hey."

Reluctantly, Ellie straightened when she heard a familiar voice.

"I swear I won't bother you for long," Bethany said. "I just needed to see with my own eyes that nothing can keep down badass Jordan Carpenter for long."

"Well, you can see I'm still down for the time being, but it looks like I'll live."

"That's what I wanted to hear. Ellie, there's someone here for you."

It took Ellie a moment to decipher Bethany's pointed look at her. "Okay, sure. I'll be back in a few minutes."

Ellie went to see her visitor, nearly groaning at the sight of the man in the long coat. She didn't know him well, but she'd seen him around before: IA investigator Rob Garcia.

"Detective Harding." He shook her hand. "I'm aware these aren't the best circumstances, but I thought you'd appreciate if we do this as quickly as possible, just to check all the boxes. You mind if we go to the cafeteria for a moment?"

Bethany was doing her another favor. It was easy to get irritated with her sometimes, hard to stay mad at her for long. Ellie wasn't always sure if she was still trying to make amends for one consequential mistake, or what else her reason was to act like she did.

Today, she was grateful.

"Sure, let's go."

They sat down at a table by the window. "I talked to my lieutenant already, and apologized. I didn't touch that woman. All I wanted was a couple of minutes to talk to her."

"Why?" he asked.

"Why? You really can't imagine?"

"Honestly? Yes, I'm having a bit of trouble understanding. You worked on the case, you know how fucked up the whole deal was that the women on the inside got, and that Joy Anne Deane was one of those who helped facilitate the abuse. I would think your sole motivation was that she'd be held accountable for what she did, then and especially now."

"You'll recommend suspension?"

Ellie was more angry than worried, though this would be the worst possible time. Most of all, she was angry at herself, for letting herself cross that line.

"All those cops out there in the waiting room, they would have liked to have a word with her. They didn't," Garcia pointed out.

"Jordan is my wife!" Ellie took a deep breath, reminding herself that he was not the enemy. "I'm sorry. Lieutenant Carroll already read me the riot act. I get it. But frankly, neither he nor you know what it's like. The brothers and women like Joy Anne might be extreme, but a lot of people believe what they believe."

"I'm not arguing, Detective. My only concern is that you are able to do your job, and that a lapse of judgment like today is not going to happen again."

"Check all boxes, huh?" she asked wryly.

"Can I?"

"Yes, you can. I need to take care of my family. I'll do my job, and I'll let my colleagues do theirs."

"Fair enough. Thank you, Detective."

Bethany was gone by the time Ellie returned to the room. Ellie wouldn't put it past her to tell Jordan about the day's events, and frankly, she didn't care. Jordan didn't mention it though, and so she saw no reason to bring it up. She sat back down and held Jordan's hand in hers. Being torn into every which direction, she needed to feel connected.

"You don't have to spend all your time here."

"Pauline is with Meri. And everyone else understands. Don't worry about anything."

Something about Jordan's expression alarmed her.

"Are you in pain? Should I get the nurse?"

"No. Please don't."

Ellie wasn't reassured, but she also didn't want to prod. The medical staff seemed content with the progress so far, reason to be grateful. At the same time, this was a painful setback for Jordan.

"All right. I'll tell Ariel that she can come visit in a couple of days?"

"Of course. What about Meri? Could you sneak her in for a couple of minutes?" Her tone was so hopeful Ellie couldn't bring herself to crush that hope. With Jordan still being vulnerable, it wasn't a good idea for either of them. She might be able to come home at the end of the next week, but that felt like an eternity. For both of them.

"We'll see. I can probably do that."

A sin of omission, a likely lie—Ellie wasn't proud of herself, but she'd do whatever was best for Jordan's recovery. This was priority.

# Chapter Eight

A s time went by, Jordan was struck with a puzzling dilemma. She wanted things to go back to normal as soon as possible. It also meant that Ellie had to leave the hospital room for longer periods of time. On top of taking care of Meri and their home, she was checking in with her colleagues and preparing her own return to work. They had to move forward.

Yet, Jordan felt like she was falling into a deep dark pit every time Ellie left the room. She wasn't well, and "normal" would take a lot more time than she wanted it to. Not having seen Meri for the longest time since her birth depressed her too.

Jordan knew she had reason to be grateful, for being alive, for the many people who cared about her, but if she was honest, she didn't feel like seeing anyone but Ellie and Meri.

Being able to see her daughter, if only for a few minutes, would do wonders for her morale, even with the pain medication wearing off.

❧

With about four hours of sleep, half of them in the visitor's chair, Ellie once more had a quick breakfast with Pauline, before she headed to the station, another day at the hospital planned afterwards. Becca Crane would come by later with Ariel.

"Thank you so much," she said after practically inhaling the hot coffee. "I don't know what I'd do without you."

"We're family." Pauline hesitated long enough for Ellie to worry. No doubt, she worried a lot these days, about anything that might disturb the fragile equilibrium she'd achieved since it was clear that Jordan would make a full recovery. She'd handled Joy Anne and IA, but she didn't think she could bear any more bad news.

"There's something else on your mind."

"You look exhausted, Ellie. You need to sleep more."

"Come on, like anyone *could* sleep right now. I need to be with Jordan and our child as much as I can, and I need to figure something out about the job. I'm fine."

"They're taking good care of her. You have to take care of yourself too."

"I think you're doing a great job of that. I'm okay, really."

"You want me to come by when Ariel visits? Jack can take over, and Kate will be here this evening."

"I think we'll be good. Dr. Crane will come with Ariel, and that means it will already a bit crowded. If you'd like to come this evening, I'll stay here with Meri and Kate."

"Sure. We'll figure it out."

They hugged quickly, then Ellie was on her way. She wondered if Cameron would take her off the task force, and frankly, she didn't have any objections. It would probably be easier for everyone if she returned to her unit and desk once Jordan was home.

Ellie could have gone straight to the task force's office, but she wanted to spend a moment with her colleagues and see where they were on Joy Anne's case. IA didn't want her to go near the woman—she wouldn't.

Walking past a conference room, she stopped when she noticed Bethany sitting at the table with A.D.A. Valerie Esposito. Valerie saw her and got up, waving her in. She opened the door to Ellie.

"Hi, come on in for a second. How's Jordan?"

"Better every day. I promise I won't bother you for long. I just wanted to know where we are." Aware of Bethany's curious expression, she added, "I talked to IA. I know I shouldn't have gone into the room."

"No, you shouldn't have," Valerie agreed, "but that doesn't mean we can't talk. I'm going to need to sit down with you anyway, everyone who worked on the Prophets' case."

"I'll get you a coffee," Bethany offered. Ellie didn't want to stay that long, but Bethany was already at the door.

"Thanks."

It crossed her mind that both of these women had been in a relationship with Jordan once, not that it mattered in this context. They would all do whatever possible so Joy Anne would be punished.

"I don't have much time now."

"I understand, but we should do this soon. I remember well how she acted in the courtroom, yelling and screaming at the women who testified against the Prophets. You have some additional insights."

"Sure...But I think the case against her is pretty open and shut, isn't it?"

"We have that on video, yes. I'm going to charge her with a hate crime," Valerie said, the moment Bethany returned. Ellie leaned back in her seat, not sure what to say.

"Won't that be harder to prove?"

"Think about it," Bethany urged. "She knew about your and Jordan's plans to adopt Ariel. She didn't randomly target cops because CPS took her kids. Remember that homophobic rant she gave you?"

"I do, but we all know you can't use it."

"Doesn't matter." Valerie was convinced. "I have pages and pages of the same crap from when she was first arrested. We are building the case. I also went over Ariel's testimony again. She talked about how they were indoctrinated to believe anything but the abusive family structure they lived in was sick and immoral. The truth is, it could have been any of us, but she had it in it for you and Jordan especially, since you helped Ariel."

Ellie was feeling sick to her stomach—not because she might have been Joy Anne's target, but because the attack could have happened anywhere, in a place where an ambulance might have taken longer to arrive.

"Did she get any of the lawyers that originally worked for the Prophets?"

"Oh no, she wouldn't be able to afford them now. She got a public defender, a young kid barely out of law school, who is trying to shift the blame. Well, we all know who's to blame. This wasn't a spontaneous act."

"I agree." It would be absurd to suggest Joy Anne wasn't fully responsible for her actions. "I have to go now. Thanks for the coffee."

She walked over to the task force headquarters where Brigid gave her a quick update, and Ellie promised to let her know when she'd be back.

*Don't worry, Jordan. You're still my favorite. You'll always be.* Gasping for air, Jordan struggled to get into a sitting position, ignoring the pain flaring from various sources. Anything was better than being in the grip of the nightmare, the familiar voice speaking to her in a soft tone. She'd never forget that voice, even though it wasn't that much of a surprise that one maniac with a knife brought back the memory of another. But one of them was dead, and the other was facing many years in prison.

She still came out on top, didn't she?

Her gaze went to the empty chair next to the bed. It had taken some prodding, but Ellie had finally left to get a few hours of sleep at home. At this moment, Jordan wished she hadn't.

She traced her fingers over her hospital gown, remembering that other, older scar underneath. It was barely visible now, and she had stopped thinking about it—until now. She couldn't afford to go down that spiral, obsess about something that was long over. Today, her life was completely different. She had a child. A lover who wouldn't use their story as bait for a serial killer—that was hard to forget no matter how many times Bethany had apologized.

The only connection between the knife-wielding criminals was their choice of weapon and their hate. She didn't need to worry about them.

Still, Jordan found it hard to breathe, impossible to go back to sleep.

❦

In the light of day, it was easier to shake the grip of the nightmare, telling herself it was nothing but a fluke. Derek stopped by before his shift and gave her the rundown of what was going on at the station.

"You want to bring me some case files? I'm starting to get cabin fever."

"I think that's a good thing. So, when are you going home?"

"Next week, probably. I guess I'll have to schedule an appointment with Dr. Burns, and we'll go from there."

"Take the time you need. Kate and I are happy to help."

"I know, and we're grateful, but I have to work at some point, don't I?" She slumped back into the pillow with a sigh. "I'm sorry. It's impossible to get a decent amount of sleep in this place."

"I understand. We all look forward to having you back. I'll see you soon."

"Derek, wait," she called when he was already at the door. "Did Detective Carter ever get back to you about Laura Mills?"

"Oh yes, they have a suspect in custody. Serial date rapist. It's too bad he can't be charged with murder."

Irrelevant in this context, but she remembered Joy Anne Deane coming to court in a wheelchair. She had walked into traffic as well, but they had never been able to determine if that had been her own doing, or a command by the Prophets of Better Days.

"True," she agreed. "By the way, I wasn't kidding, if you need to bounce off some ideas...I feel like my brain is starting to slow down."

"I'll see what I can do. Have a good day."

# Chapter Nine

E llie remained on the task force as Brigid was nearly ready for her undercover assignment to start. For the past couple of days, she had spent a few hours at work, relieved that everyone kept their promise to give her the time she needed—only because Jordan all but chased her from the room.

"Remember that we have a kid at home and a mortgage to pay. Sooner or later, one of us has to bring home some money."

It was hard to argue with that. "You'll be bringing in some money soon, but I see your point."

Today, however, she wouldn't go in. Today was the day Jordan was released from the hospital, taking home an abundance of flowers and get-well cards, and other gifts.

Jack and Pauline would be waiting at home and staying for dinner. After all their support, this was the least Ellie could do.

"You're good?" she asked after Jordan had fastened her seatbelt.

"Yes. Perfect."

"You're sure?" While there was no visible sign of her recent ordeal, she looked pale and tired.

"You can't stay parked here for long," Jordan pointed out. "And yes, I really want to go home. I've never been so sure of anything."

"Okay, let's go. There are people waiting for us."

"People?"

Ellie smiled at Jordan's panicked look. "Three people, to be exact, and your parents won't stay long. Everyone else will give it a little time."

"You scared me there."

"I know. I'm sorry."

"Never mind. Thank you so much for handling it all."

Ellie reached over to take her hand. There was nothing to say. She had done what was necessary. There was no point in bringing up thoughts that sprang up every once in a while—like the question why Derek had been the first Jordan thought to call. Both he and Ellie had handled their part. No need to discuss it.

At the house, she carefully watched Jordan going up the porch stairs.

"Stop it. I can walk."

However, Ellie saw her wince, when, a moment later, Pauline opened the door and embraced her carefully.

"Welcome home," she said warmly. "We've set up in the living room. All you have to do is get comfortable."

Jack waited until Jordan sat on the couch before he handed a sleepy Meri to her. Jordan held her tightly, and it was Ellie's turn to wince—for both of them. But this time, the tears were happy ones.

Being at home, sleeping in her own bed, was a huge improvement. A time or two, after waking from a nightmare, Jordan had snuck out of bed and calmed her nerves by watching Meri sleep. Ellie slept on too, testimony to how much had rested on her shoulders these past weeks. Jordan saw no reason to tell her about the nightmares, because she knew from experience, they would fade. Things would, had to, get back to normal sometime, even though she found it hard to pinpoint that moment.

Being parents had disrupted their routines in various ways, most of them welcome, some of them challenging.

She'd lived through another close call, and Jordan's most important coping strategy had always been to go back to work as soon as possible. She hadn't made the appointment with the department psychiatrist yet. Jordan wasn't sure why, but it meant spending more time with the most amazing child that had ever existed. That was a good reason, wasn't it?

Ellie had been back at work for a while now. She brought up the subject over breakfast.

"Everyone keeps asking about you," she said. "They really miss you."

"I know. My cell phone doesn't stop."

"They care."

Pushing her cup out of Meri's curious reach, she said, "I know. No, sweetie, you can't have that."

It looked like the baby was pouting, making her laugh. Funny it seemed Meri looked so much more like Ellie than herself.

"You don't have to go back right away, but why not get the paperwork out of the way?" Ellie suggested. "I know you hate that the most."

"I'll figure something out with Dr. Burns," Jordan said. "I just need a bit of catching up with the little one."

Ellie smiled. "I know. You think you two could do me a favor and get some pasta? I would cook tonight, but I don't know if I have time to run by the store."

"Of course."

"Awesome. I'll have to go in a minute, but first, I need kisses."

⌘

She'd been better, physically, so she wondered if this was a good time to restart the habit of going to the coffee shop with Meri after buying a few things for dinner. So many things had changed—familiarity was a good thing. Jordan was quickly reminded of her limitations when someone behind her waiting to get into the store stood a little too close.

"Can't you see this is going to take a freaking second?" she snapped at the twenty-something woman who took a hasty step backwards.

"Sorry," she mumbled. "No need to yell."

Inside the store, a man was holding the door open, but seeing the tears already forming in Meri's eyes, Jordan backed away. "No thanks."

Meri was starting to cry in earnest, giving Jordan little time to examine what had happened. Not that she needed a shrink to explain it to her. The young woman coming up a little too close behind her was simply impatient, not a violent criminal with a knife.

"Come on, no need to cry. Mommy's fine. We're both fine."

A more cynical part of her questioned that statement. She stepped aside and took Meri out of her stroller, rocking her.

Prep time was coming to an end, with Brigid only days away from entering the correctional facility. Her main objective was to find out how the drugs that killed the two inmates, had found their way into the prison.

Even though Ellie had plenty to worry about outside of the job, she wasn't immune to the rising tension within the group. Everyone was laser focused on their task.

Before the end of her shift, she got herself a coffee and brought one for Brigid who sat at her desk, studying some files. Ellie knew she had memorized their content already.

Looking up at the offered treat, Brigid smiled.

"Thank you. I'm going to miss you when you go back to Homicide."

"I don't know about that, but thanks."

Ellie hesitated for a few heartbeats. She had done some undercover work, but those were usually short-term assignments, opportunities—or necessities—springing up at a last moment's notice. This was a different story, Brigid preparing to adopt her undercover persona, fulfilling an assignment that might take longer than they imagined.

"Are you scared?" she asked.

Brigid regarded her, probably understanding that there was a bigger context to Ellie's question.

"A little fear is a healthy thing to have," she said. "Keeps you on your toes. I believe we'll figure out what happened, and I'll be back with my family soon. I'm aware there's a risk. But we believe that the work matters, right?"

"Yes, we do."

Juggling the importance of family and the job was something very present on her mind these days—especially confronted with Jordan's dilemma.

"Anyway," she added, "Good luck. Have a good evening."

"You too...and Ellie?"

Already on her way out, Ellie turned around.

"Don't mind Cameron. He can be a little intense, but he's one of the good guys. And he gets the job done."

"That's the impression I got," Ellie said. "Good night."

Ellie came home to a quiet house—naptime. She felt a bit torn these days, relieved to know that Jordan was home taking care of Meri, but also anxious. Perhaps she was projecting a bit, because Jordan had to be anxious to go back to work. She always was, even after a planned and wished for time-out. Ellie remembered being surprised seeing her back so soon after the Darby case. It was just the way she was.

Intent on starting dinner, she opened the pantry door, suppressing a sigh when she didn't see any pasta. She inspected the fridge next, coming up empty once more. Ellie had let it go, once, twice. She didn't want to cause drama over one missing item when they could just order in like the other times. Truth be told, she felt bad asking Jordan for those little errands, even aware that her reluctance was irrational.

"Oh hey, you're here." Jordan's apologetic expression told her the same subject was on her mind. "I'm really sorry. I forgot. Can we order in?"

"Sure." She opened a drawer and took out the takeout menus. "Did you call Dr. Burns?"

"You'd like a play by play of my day?" There was a slight edge to her voice. Ellie resisted the sudden impulse to put more force than necessary behind the drawer. They were both tired, but grateful. So grateful. They'd always find a way to navigate the rockier waters, and this was nothing.

"Sure, but I'm really hungry. Let me order first, and I can have a quick shower before they arrive."

Jordan didn't object to any of it, but the instant relief showing in her composure was disconcerting to Ellie. They would have to have that conversation soon.

Kate called, and they made plans for dinner the next weekend. Afterwards, Ellie turned off her phone. She decided not to make forgotten groceries an issue, when they could have dishes prepared by an Italian chef delivered to their door. They made it an early night, knowing from experience that it might be wise to get some sleep while they could. Meri was sleeping through most nights now, though she'd be awake and ready to start the day early.

Ellie woke a few hours later, realizing Jordan was awake as well. 2:47 and quietude.

"Did you sleep at all?" she wondered out loud.

"A bit. Now you do the same. You'll have to be up early tomorrow."

"I'll be okay." Ellie sat up, studying her wife until Jordan looked away, uncomfortable with the scrutiny.

"Good."

"I think we need to talk."

"About what? You're still mad about the pasta?"

"I'm not mad. I just wonder..." Was there any way to say this and not make her sound ungrateful? "You haven't talked much about what your plan is. I swear I'll support you whatever you want to do, but I need to know." She watched the mixed emotions flicker over Jordan's face, trying to interpret each of them.

"There's nothing to talk about. I'll go back to work soon. I'll just have to clear it with the doc."

"Are you sure?"

"What do you want me to say? I didn't get around to making the call. I'll do it tomorrow, if that eases your mind. Can we go back to sleep now?"

"Please, don't do this. If you'd like to stay home with Meri longer, I understand. We can make it work."

"Let's talk about it another time. I'm tired."

Ellie acknowledged that they wouldn't finish this conversation tonight. Jordan turned away, but she let herself be embraced.

# Chapter Ten

Ellie had checked in with her colleagues, indicating that she was willing to work as much overtime as it took to make up for her prolonged absence...but she needed this morning. Not to push, but to remind both of them where they stood.

"I thought you had to go in early." Jordan looked surprised and a tad wary when she entered the kitchen where Ellie had set the table. Meri was next to her in her highchair.

"I didn't mean to blindside you, but I took a half day."

"Isn't that sort of the opposite of what we said we'd do?"

"It's important. I have been so...terrified, I'm afraid I didn't pay enough attention."

"You've been working," Jordan pointed out. "Taking care of Meri when I couldn't."

"But you have these past weeks, even when it was hard for you. Harder than I imagined."

Jordan poured both of them a coffee before she sat down and picked up her cup, then set it down again.

"I know you'd like to make sense of this somehow. I don't know if I can help you with that. I'm sorry."

"What is it that you're afraid of? I'm here for you. Whatever you need."

"I wish I knew. It's not the same this time."

"What isn't?"

"Groceries...Work? The truth is I haven't made the call because I don't know what the result will be. How can I protect anyone if I can't even handle going to the store? If I'm not sure Dr. Burns sure as hell won't be."

Ellie was starting to have a better picture. Perhaps she had been in denial, wanting to go back to the larger plan so badly. They'd lived through close calls before, and going back to blessed routine had been a lifesaver. Not for Kate, though. She had made big changes.

"It's perfectly normal to feel the way you do. And I meant what I said. We have time to figure it out."

"I don't know about normal." Jordan toyed with a piece of toast on her plate. "She's a confused twenty-something year old, for Christ's sake."

"A twenty-something year old with a knife, driven by hate. But she doesn't matter to me. You do. All I'm asking is for you to think about whether you want to talk to someone other than me...postpone Dr. Burns for a bit, or indefinitely. Whatever it is, I'm with you. I won't judge. And frankly, no one else will, because they know I could shoot them."

Jordan chuckled at that, though her eyes were welling up.

"It's been rough. But I don't know that I'd even be here without you."

"My point exactly. You're not without me. And—" Ellie's cell phone started vibrating on the table. "You've got to be kidding me. Not now."

"It's okay. I got it covered here."

"I told them I'd come in later." Ellie sighed. "How about we go for groceries tomorrow night? I think we'll manage until then. We still have enough diapers, at least."

The phone rang.

"Come on, pick it up," Jordan urged, and reluctantly, she did.

"Harding." Jordan had directed her attention to Meri, but her smile told Ellie that her irritation had shown in her tone.

"Harding, this is Cameron. I'm sorry, but we need you to come in."

"This really can't wait an hour?"

It was true, nothing was the same. Neither of them had ever questioned putting the job first. At this moment Ellie did.

"No, it can't. Brigid called. She's in the hospital."

"What? Why?"

She became aware of both Jordan and Meri regarding her with worry.

"She had an accident, driver hit her bike. She's got a broken leg and a concussion."

Ellie wasn't sure whether to sigh in relief or curse. This wasn't a good outcome by any means, but it could always be worse.

"I'll be there as soon as I can. I assume the assignment is off?"

"That's what we need to talk about. I'll see you when you get here."

Before she could react, he ended the call.

"I am so ready for this assignment to be over," she said to Jordan. "I think it will be soon, for me anyway."

"I can't say I'm sad about it. Everything okay?"

"Brigid had an accident with her bike. Looks like she'll be okay, but she can't go in now. My guess is that we'll call everything off and try to find a different angle, but Carroll will want me to come back to my desk eventually. At least I hope he does."

"Of course. And you can go. Meri and I will find something to do with the day."

"I love you." Ellie leaned forward to kiss her. "We'll get back to this, I promise."

She was almost out the door when the bell rang, not sure how she felt about seeing Kathryn standing in front of it with a couple of grocery bags.

In the briefing room, Ellie couldn't help stealing glances at her watch. Cameron was still on the phone, the other members of the task force, all men, standing around the table. She liked them all well enough, but the timing was off—even though Jordan had assured her in a whisper it was fine to go. They had a few things they needed to tackle, so she'd never gotten around to tell Jordan about Kathryn's offer. She hoped Kathryn would be able to see the situation for what it was, a time to tread carefully.

"All right," Cameron said after he'd ended the call. "We don't have a lot of time. Brigid is out for the time being, but fortunately, we have an option. We can delay a few days, but not much longer. Ellie, what do you think?"

Since the call, Ellie had been worried something like this might happen, and she'd hoped she'd be wrong.

"Can't we postpone until Brigid is back? Or send someone else?"

"Whoever is responsible for the women's deaths will have a lot of time to cover their tracks if we don't act now. So, the answer to your first question is no, as for the second, that would be you. You have all the information that Brigid has."

And, he didn't need to say it out loud, she was the only woman besides Brigid, the logical choice. Any other day, Ellie wouldn't have hesitated, not much anyway. She would still want to run something potentially so consequential by Jordan. This wasn't any other day. "That is true, though...Could I talk to you in private for a moment?"

"Guys, give us the room?"

When they were alone, Ellie said, "I know that I have the same facts, but this is a big deal."

He studied her calmly. "I know. Everyone knows. People around here have heard your name before. I wouldn't be suggesting this if I thought you couldn't handle it."

"Thank you. I know it's important, but the timing is really bad."

"I'm sorry. I don't see much of an alternative."

"Can I have some time to think about it?"

"Twenty-four hours, then I'll have to call the boss and tell him all this prep was for nothing, and we're starting at square one."

That wasn't entirely fair, since some of the detectives had followed other avenues. He'd be right to say that they hadn't been able to turn up much, yet. Brigid's plan had been the most promising so far.

"I'm sorry, too, but I don't think I can do it." She and Jordan had barely started to examine the aftermath of the attack. She couldn't leave her alone. Frankly, she didn't want to.

"Like you said, it's a big deal. Go over everything. Talk to Brigid again if you have to. Talk to your wife and let me know tomorrow afternoon."

"Thank you for giving me that time. I'll do that, but don't expect my answer to be any different."

"We'll see," Cameron said.

❦

"I heard that Ellie's back at work, so I thought you'd have your hands full with my favorite granddaughter."

Jordan decided she was too tired to listen for any sort of hidden motive in Kathryn's statement, but she watched carefully when Kathryn lifted Meri out of her chair.

"Hello beautiful! It's amazing," she said. "They change so much in such a short time."

"They do. You want a coffee? I think it's still hot."

"That would be great, but please, sit. I can get it myself. First, I should put these away." She indicated the bags with groceries. "I thought I could make you lunch today. Or dinner, depending on what you feel like."

"You didn't have to do that."

"Oh yes, I did." Kathryn didn't elaborate, and Jordan didn't ask her to.

"All right. Thanks. But I can pour a cup of coffee."

She did while Kathryn stored away her purchases and sat down with Meri in her lap. The baby's sudden movement caused a jolt of pain, nerves, she'd been told, something to be expected. If Kathryn had noticed a minute change in her expression, she didn't mention it.

"I'm so happy to see you back on your feet," she said. "How are you doing? You're thinking of going back to work?"

It seemed like everyone needed an answer to that question *right now*. Ellie, of course, had a right to know. Jordan wasn't sure this was true for anyone else, but she didn't want to expand the subject.

"Sure."

"You know you can call me whenever you need me."

"Thank you. That's very kind." It didn't mean she had to or would call. Their changing relationship was still fragile in parts, enough for Jordan to want to monitor Kathryn's presence in Meri's life closely. "How have you been?"

"We've been good. Jim and I might be moving into an apartment soon. But I can see you're tired. Why don't you take a nap while I clean up here? I can watch Meri meanwhile."

"Thank you, but I think she could use a nap too."

To her surprise, Jordan fell asleep minutes after her head hit the pillow, the sounds from the kitchen luring her into a dreamless and surprisingly restful sleep. No nightmares. No worries that Ellie might find out about all the things on the list that didn't get done. She still hadn't made the call, but there was no hurry, right?

She left the bedroom to find Kathryn with Meri in the living room, on a blanket on the floor.

"What did you do?" The question was as unnecessary as her tone. Jordan could see that the stack of dishes had disappeared from the counter. Meri had woken from her nap before her, and she sported new clothes, and, possibly, a new diaper.

"I didn't want to wake you," Kathryn said, clearly understanding every nuance and implication. "I know I wasn't very good at this back then, but I've been helping Serena with her baby a lot. You remember Serena?"

"I do."

Ironic that Kathryn taking care of things alarmed her, when in the first years of her life, Kathryn's lack of caring for anything but drugs and alcohol had been the problem.

"Next time, wake me."

Kathryn nodded, perhaps drawing hope from the idea that there might be a next time. Already, Jordan wished Ellie could come home, Derek having an urgent question about a case a close second.

# Chapter Eleven

No way in hell. That wasn't what she'd said to Cameron, or in her brief conversation with Carroll on the way out. Ellie would visit Brigid another time, but she didn't need to ask her advice on accepting the assignment or not. If people knew her name, she was in the lucky position of being able to say no, and that would be her answer, today and the next day.

The words she and Jordan exchanged the previous night and this morning were still too vivid on her mind. Ellie was aware they might not come to a conclusion in twenty-four hours, but this mattered to her. Jordan and Meri, and their well-being mattered to her before anything else, and no flattery from supervisors would change that.

When Ellie let herself into the house, she saw Kathryn's coat on the rack, unsure what to make of the fact that she was still there. Things looked calm, the table in the kitchen set for two.

"Hi Ellie. Dinner is ready. Jim is coming to get me—oh, here he is." Kathryn gave a quick hug to Jordan and kissed Meri's cheek. "Like I said, any time. Sit, please, I can let myself out."

She was grateful that it would be just the two of them, and tired already, but there was one thing she had to do before sitting down. Jordan went into her embrace eagerly.

"Okay." Ellie stepped back a bit quicker than she'd intended, the intensity of emotion catching her off guard. "Let's eat. That was nice of Kathryn, right? How was your day?"

"Quiet," Jordan said. "What about you? You left pretty quickly this morning."

"Yeah. They're going to have to make some changes...Now that Brigid is out, they want me to go in. I said no, of course." When Jordan didn't answer right away, she added, "This is the part where I hoped you'd say, this is a good decision. Because it is. We can't do this right now, and that's okay."

"If you're okay with it, I am too."

"There's no 'if.' It's the right thing to do."

"It's a big opportunity, and a vote of confidence that they asked you, rather than scrap the whole operation. Have you talked to Brigid?"

"I don't need to, not about that. I'll visit her sometime this week when I have time."

"What did Cameron say?"

Ellie was tempted to take a shortcut so they could end the subject but decided against it. Despite all of the challenges, they were in a good place. No room for secrets.

"He gave me twenty-four hours to think about it. I've thought about it. I don't want to go. They can't fire me over that. It was never supposed to be me."

"No one's talking about firing. You don't have to turn them down because of me."

"It's for us," Ellie insisted. "This was interesting, but honestly I look forward to being back at my own desk."

"Me too." Jordan's smile was genuine, affirming to Ellie that she'd been correct in her assessment.

After dinner, they retreated to the living room. The last thing Jordan wanted was for Ellie to go on a high-risk undercover assignment when she had only little time to switch gears. There was not a doubt in her mind that she was up to the task. Since her return to the task force, she'd brought herself up to speed on the latest developments. While Jordan didn't know all the details, she was aware that there had been a second murder. High risk. Potentially high profile. Those deaths might be random tragic occurrences, but they might just as well shine a light on practices in one particular prison, and flaws in the correctional system as a whole. Her thoughts were wandering, and Ellie had noticed when they watched the news together.

"Where are you?" Ellie asked softly.

Perhaps she was right, they, too had a right to pull back and think of their own lives and family first, if only for a while. But it was hard to pinpoint the moment. Those victims deserved justice too, and whether the investigators probed a different angle or trained someone new, it would take more time and money. Jordan suppressed a sigh. It would have been smart, too, to assign more women to the group when the crime scene to be investigated was a women's correctional facility.

"Right here, with you."

"I know you have doubts. I don't."

"I'm not doubting you. I'll support your decision either way. I just—" It was hard to express how she felt both happy and selfish about Ellie's approach.

"I get it. But I'll still go to work. The difference is I'll come home at the end of the day. If things were different...but they aren't, and right now I can't wait to get back. They get our situation."

If Ellie could be rational about this, so could she, right?

"They do."

Ellie sat back, pulling her legs up under her. "Okay. If I didn't know better, I'd almost think you want me to go."

"No."

"I know this matters, the women matter, and the resources put into the task force. I'm sure Brigid is having a hard time, but honestly, that's not on my mind right now. We have a baby to take care of. I almost lost you. This is all I can think about." She didn't raise her voice, but each of her words hit home. "Maybe I don't care about the job as much as I thought I did."

"I know you care. It's been a lot." Jordan pulled her close, thinking that projecting her own emotions onto Ellie's situation might be the selfish part. Ellie was right. They had earned the right to say no—but there was something more to consider. Jordan chided herself for considering this earlier in their conversation. "And speaking of which. You've worked a few high-profile cases. Natalie found you because of them."

"Someone else might too," Ellie said. "That makes me look a lot less selfish, doesn't it?"

"I never thought you were, but it's something Cameron needs to consider. Your name might have come up in connection with Joy Anne Deane and the Prophets."

"You're brilliant. Did I mention I love you?"

All of a sudden, it was easier to breathe.

❦

To Ellie's surprise, Lieutenant Carroll was present at her meeting with Cameron, standing at the back of the room, arms crossed over his chest.

"Don't mind me," he said. "As you know, we've had a few unexpected incidents in the past few weeks. I'd just like to know when I'll have my detective back."

"Sooner than later, I think," Ellie answered, proud that her voice didn't waver. She was used to making her case in a group of more experienced colleagues—and she knew her points were valid. "I swear I've given this a lot of thought, and I talked to Jordan as well. My name has been in the local paper a few times lately, the last time when a former member of the Prophets attacked my wife. It's reasonable to assume that someone in that prison might be aware. My cover likely wouldn't last."

"One local paper," Cameron said. "Come on."

"You really want to take that risk?" She saw his face reddening, while Carroll looked like he was suppressing a smirk.

"Harding, this is not my first time. I would never recklessly put anyone in my team in danger. Two women are dead!"

"I'm aware. And I'm sorry, I can't help you."

She wondered if Cameron had asked Carroll to join in order to sway her. Her supervisor was aware of the status of her assignment every step of the way. He didn't need to be in the meeting for it.

"I think Detective Harding has a point. I'd like to see her back at her desk come Monday morning."

Ellie took a deep breath, though her relief didn't last long.

Cameron shook his head. "Lieutenant, with all due respect...There has been a new development in the case. A guard who has been working for the facility for the past six years has disappeared."

"What? And you didn't tell me?"

"I was going to once you were done with your speech."

"I think I've heard enough," Lt. Carroll said. "Detective Harding, could you leave us alone? This won't take long."

Ellie had no choice but to follow his request. She waited outside the briefing room for a nail-biting four and a half minutes, before Carroll came out, his expression unreadable.

"Sir, I wanted to apologize for making this so complicated."

"It's not your fault it became complicated. I'll see you Monday morning."

Apprehensive and curious in equal parts, Ellie went back into the room where Cameron sat brooding over a file. She carefully closed the door behind her.

"Well, it looks like you got your wish," he said, tossing the file to her. "We're going to the prison tomorrow, interviews with staff and inmates. Again. You better get ready."

"What about the missing guard?"

"Didn't I make myself clear? I want you to be up to date by tomorrow morning. It looks like you won't grace us with your presence much longer, so we better make the best of it, right?"

While she didn't like his attitude, Ellie barely suppressed an inappropriate smile. The next few days would come with long hours, and there might be some awkwardness, but she could finally see that light at the end of the tunnel.

⁕

Jordan picked up the phone, hesitating. There was a fair chance that Cameron might try to guilt Ellie into taking the assignment anyway. He had given her something akin to an ultimatum, after all. She couldn't deny it would make a difference, because this wasn't a matter of just two or three days.

"Let's hope we came up with some good points, right?" She tickled Meri's cheek and got some happy, life-affirming laughter in response. Meri had been quieter in the past weeks. It was scary to realize how perceptive small children were, picking up everything going on around them—good and bad.

Her cell phone vibrated on the table, and Meri stretched out her hands.

The moment of truth. Ellie's quick text message only said, *I'll have to work late, but the assignment is off*. With a heart emoji.

She'd never thought Ellie not getting a job would fill her with this much relief.

"Okay, it's already a good day. What are we going to do with the rest of it? You're up for a walk to the coffee shop with Mommy?"

Jordan really wanted to make that call, though she'd have to test her ability to deal with the general public some more—if she wanted to continue to serve and protect said public.

# Chapter Twelve

E llie wasn't sure if her presence would be absolutely necessary, or some sort of punishment, but she'd do her job
well. Members of the task force had interviewed Gaines' and
Webber's cell mates, and the women on their block. Ellie had
practically memorized the transcripts.

A number of guards were assigned to each block, though they
sometimes traded shifts.

She hadn't spoken to any of the people in question, though
that would change tomorrow, and she had to be prepared.

With Cameron watching her like a hawk, she had no opportunity to slip out and visit Brigid, but she studied every piece of
paper until the letters started to blur in front of her eyes. She
talked to every member of the task force who had been inside
the prison.

When she put on her coat and picked up the car keys,
Cameron came up behind her.

"Ready?" he asked.

"Yes."

"Look, I'm sorry about earlier. There's been a lot of pressure.
Politicians are starting to realize that this is an issue, and more
people are paying attention."

"We all should be," she said. "Thank you for understanding."

"It's fine. You did good work here."

"Thanks. I'll see you tomorrow."

"Don't be late."

Ellie didn't think she had to respond. She was relieved that they seemed to be on the same page, wanting to keep the tension to a minimum while they wrapped up their work together.

Her mood improved even further when she came home to the delicious smells of a dinner on the stove.

"It's almost ready. I started when you texted you were on your way."

"This is awesome, thank you."

"No, it's something I should have been thinking about a while ago." Jordan obviously wasn't talking about the stir-fry any longer. "You've had a lot to deal with. So—today we finally made it to the store."

"That's good. And it smells yummy."

"That was the easy part. I'll go in to make an appointment with Dr. Burns tomorrow."

"Are you sure? I'll be back with Homicide on Monday. No one will question it if you take some more time."

"I think it will be harder the more time I take. I have to do this at least."

Ellie stepped forward to kiss her. "If this feels right to you, I'm with you."

"Thank you. Now let's eat before it gets cold."

Ellie was beyond relieved that she wouldn't have to spend weeks locked up starting days from today—instead, she'd spend a long tedious day, perhaps a couple, asking the same questions once more, but she could live with that. It already felt like an occasion to celebrate, even if she had to get up early the next day.

She wasn't fooling herself, knowing they still had ways to go...but like always, they would make it.

In the bedroom, after the babycam was activated, she pulled Jordan close to her.

"I know we're both tired, and the weekend is still pretty far away, but maybe we could find another way to relax..."

Jordan's smile sent a familiar, welcome shiver down her spine. Ellie wasn't sure how she'd receive her suggestion. She had anticipated that adding a new member to the family would change dynamics, and she thought they had done pretty well...But neither of them had raised the subject in some time.

"I just want to be close to you," she whispered. "If that's okay with you."

"I want that too."

Jordan spoke without hesitation, though she reached over to turn off the lights. If she was more comfortable that way, Ellie was all for it.

"Don't worry," Jordan said. "I'll find you." The warm hand traveling up her thigh was proof, though Ellie felt she had to make something clear.

"I know you will..." The "but" lingered unspoken.

"Let it go, just for tonight, okay?"

"You don't have to be self-conscious with me. You had a baby, and you've been through so much. As far as I'm concerned, you're Wonder Woman. You're the most beautiful person I know." Damn it, she was going to make herself cry. This was not the kind of mood she had envisioned.

"I hear you. And I appreciate you saying that, but please, stop talking." The deep messy kiss distracted Ellie for a while, and she gave in, certain that her message had been received.

"I meant it though." And then, words eluded her.

⁓⧫⁓

Ellie hadn't slept this well in a long time, even though it felt too short when Jordan kissed her awake.

"I hate to do this, but you said something about not giving Cameron another opportunity to be a jerk."

"Yes. Damn," she cursed, pushing back the covers. "I'm never late!"

"You won't be," Jordan assured her. "Breakfast will be ready after your shower."

"Meri?"

"Still asleep, but her breakfast will be ready too."

"Okay, thank you. I better get going. Wow. You're dressed already, and I slept through all of it."

"Wonder Woman, remember?"

"Am I going to regret this?" Ellie wondered out loud, though she had to admit she was happy to hear the familiar confidence in Jordan's tone. She had reason for it too.

"Hurry up," Jordan said, amused. "Otherwise, you *are* going to be late."

That was the last thing Ellie wanted.

Pauline arrived on time to babysit Meri. Jordan didn't expect to stay long at the department. She thought showing up in person would make a difference. Once Dr. Burns had put her in the calendar, she couldn't back out, could she? If anything, she'd be able to see how far she could get out of her comfort zone. So far, so good. Ellie had taken the car for a cleaning, a more symbolic gesture since there hadn't been much blood on it.

With the sun shining brightly, and the radio playing, the incident, and the dark and dreary days afterwards seemed unreal, which was fine with Jordan. She wasn't sure when she'd begun to refer to the violent act as the incident. The neutral, less emotional term made her feel less helpless, less like the victim. She needed that, especially today.

Everyone kept reminding her that she'd made it through traumatic events before, and maybe it was time to accept that. It was over. Joy Anne Deane would spend a long time behind bars, the only unfortunate outcome that some would still see her as a martyr.

Faced with the choice between the lot and the parking garage, Jordan chose the latter. Lightning didn't strike twice, right? She was aware of the rising tension gripping her body, her fingers tightening on the steering wheel. That was normal. It wasn't like going to the store, or the coffee shop. But she had lived for months in a house sold to her by a man who turned out to be a serial killer.

Jordan found a parking spot near an elevator, on a different level than that last time. Most of her colleagues were probably out on a case. All she had to do was go in, quick, say hello, stop by Dr. Burns' office and get out. Jordan sat unmoving, her hands on the wheel, forcing herself to take slow, measured breaths.

A little fear was a good thing. It kept you from being careless.

This...wasn't good. She contemplated backing out and leaving, coming back another day. Feeling cold and clammy all over, she reached over to open the door, got out and locked the car. She headed for the elevator door. When Jordan stepped out on her floor, the lightheadedness wasn't entirely gone, but she didn't feel like running anymore. For now.

Dr. Burns came out to greet her between sessions. "Detective Carpenter," she said, smiling brightly. "It's good to see you."

"You too, Doc. And no, that wasn't sarcastic."

"I didn't think it was. How are you doing?"

"Well, I'm here. I wanted to make an appointment so we could go over...the usual stuff." Except this had been far from the usual.

"Of course. I'm afraid I don't have much time this morning, but Sally can give you an appointment." Behind her desk, Sally nodded encouragingly.

"That works for me. Thanks."

# Chapter Thirteen

T he guard stood in the corner as Ellie and Cameron sat across from Jane McAdams who had shared a cell with Patty Gaines.

"I told your people before, I didn't talk much to her. I don't know where she got the drugs, but she seemed pretty spaced out most of the time."

While she addressed Cameron, her eyes were on Ellie, something Ellie found unnerving.

"You never noticed or paid attention whom she talked to? During visits maybe?"

"If she had any visits, I don't know about them."

Ellie leaned forward. The guard stood with her back straight, watching closely.

"Would you say she was friendly with the staff?"

"What exactly do you mean by that?" Jane asked, the hint of a smile on her face. "Excuse me, I do think it's a tragedy, but your question doesn't make sense."

"Why?"

"You figure it out, honey. You go home after this. I talk too much, the same thing that happened to her, might happen to me, right?"

"Is anyone threatening you?"

The guard made a half step towards them. Jane looked over her shoulder and smiled at her. "Not yet."

"Do you know correctional officer Crystal Sherman?"

Her answer was a shrug.

"Yes or no?" Cameron asked, his patience obviously waning.

"Know is a big word. She works shifts on my block sometimes. If you suspect her of anything, forget about it. She's the worst kind of person to work in a place like this, probably cries herself to sleep every night. She's close to tears during daytime."

Ellie had the impression that Jane was enjoying the situation, confronted with someone who needed something from her—but did she really know that much?

"I'm sorry I can't help you much. But you can come visit me anytime."

"Crystal is missing. Do you have any idea what she was so upset about?"

"We don't exactly sit down for tea together," Jane said, amused.

"No, but two women have died, and a third one is missing. We want to protect you."

"Well, in that case you've been doing a shitty job so far. I appreciate you talking to me, but I don't have anything new to say. Sorry, honey."

"Detective. Harding."

"Sorry, Detective Harding," the woman drawled.

"I guess we're done here." Cameron sounded frustrated, making Ellie wonder if he was still blaming her, and if he had a point. Everyone she'd seen and talked to in here seemed so occupied with themselves. Would anyone have really recognized her from articles about Natalie, Joy Anne, or others? Would she have an easier rapport with someone like Jane McAdams if the woman thought of her as another inmate? They were running into walls. She was afraid that if they didn't find Crystal

Sherman, this would all lead to nothing. Ellie hoped Lieutenant Carroll didn't have any regrets.

⌧

"Hey. I didn't expect you here today." Derek drew her into a brief hug before he pointed to the mess on his desk. "It's great timing too. Would you, by any chance, like to give me a hand with that?"

"Wow. Officially, no. What do you have?"

"I missed you so much. Sit. What we have is a dead body. Oliver Boyd. Two days ago, he walked away from his pals during a weekend trip. College buddies found him dead at the bottom of a cliff. Parents were on vacation, they'll be here tomorrow. There is the possibility of suicide."

Jordan frowned. "Why? That doesn't sound like something a person would do while on a trip with friends."

"Those friends kept hinting that he was struggling with something, but they insist they don't know details. Here, take a look."

She opened the file and winced at the victim's yearbook picture. He was young.

"There's no sign that anyone was with him. We thought accident at first, but...The friends told us he knew the area well, was always the most careful of all of them. They can't understand why he walked away from the camp that night. He went up the path to the viewpoint, climbed over the railing and..." Derek let his words trail off, but even so, Jordan got the picture.

"I'm guessing no drugs or alcohol involved." Since she meant it to be sarcastic, Derek's answer was surprising.

"They claim he didn't drink at all that night."

87

"It looks intentional...but it could be that someone wanted to make it look that way."

"Always the optimist."

"Right. This kid is dead, nothing to be optimistic about."

"Can't argue with you on that," Derek admitted. "Would you have time to stay here for a bit? I'll buy you lunch."

"I'll have to check in with my mom, but if she can stay with Meri for a bit longer, I won't say no."

"Perfect."

Jordan took out her cell phone to make the call, her mind already on the possible avenues to follow, especially once they got to talk to the parents. Struggling with what?

It was good to be back, if only for a little while. She needed a win. If someone had pushed Oliver Boyd to his death, they'd find whoever did it.

❦

They were interrupted by a male guard who walked inside and whispered something to Cameron before he went over to his female colleague to talk to her.

"All right, I have to go. Can you finish up in here?" Cameron asked Ellie. They had three more names on the list.

"Yes, sure. What's going on?"

"It's about Sherman. I'll see you later."

"Wait!" Ellie jumped to her feet. "You're leaving? How am I going to get back into town?"

"Get a cab," he said tersely. "I have no time to discuss this now. Claim it as an expense."

She felt as left out as Jane McAdams who cast a worried look at the guards debating in the corner. Eventually, the female guard announced, "I'll show you out, Sergeant Cameron." To

Ellie, she said, "Mr. Peterson will make sure you can finish your work here."

She and Cameron left, and the man, Peterson, took her spot in the corner at the wall behind the table.

Ellie sat back down.

She hadn't missed that McAdams' posture had changed, her shoulders slumping when Peterson had walked in.

"Let's go over this one more time," Ellie said, and then the sirens started.

***

Derek skimmed over Jordan's notes before he laid them on his desk. "Wow, thank you for those. You earned your lunch."

"Funny."

"I wasn't joking. Let's go."

Jordan had mixed feelings about how her day was going, though they were mostly good ones. Perhaps she'd be back soon enough to work on this case rather than just give her impressions. It had seemed out of reach only a few days ago, but her contribution still mattered.

They took Derek's car to the restaurant, and finished their brainstorming session over the lunch menu, coffee and dessert included.

"I would definitely want to talk to the friends again," Jordan concluded. "At this age, they probably have more insights into what might have been on Oliver's mind...and I noticed you're not pointing out I'm unlikely to go see the parents. Thank you. I needed that."

"How's it going?" he asked lightly.

They'd known each other long enough that Jordan understood the gravity behind the question. Like everyone else, he was waiting to hear something concrete from her. Goals. Plans. She shrugged.

"I guess it's a good thing I still know how to do this. I made an appointment with Dr. Burns, and she'll hopefully sign the form. Business as usual."

"No one thought something like this could happen here."

"But it did. And I'd prefer not to talk about it."

"I can understand that."

"Good. If anything comes up over the weekend, you can call me."

"Be careful what you wish for. I might."

The waitress came by to refill their coffee cups the moment Derek's cell phone rang. He excused himself and got up. Jordan used the time to check in with Pauline, assuring herself that all was well at home.

"How about a slight change of plans?" Derek asked after returning to the table. "Once we're done here, I could drop you off at home and visit my Goddaughter, and we talk about Boyd some more?"

That seemed a bit too obvious. "You don't have to do that."

"What does that mean? My afternoon just fell apart, and you know I could use the help. In fact, I'd like it if the lieutenant signed up on you joining me with the parents, or at least Boyd's friends."

"That's...quick. I'd have to talk to Ellie and my parents."

"Yeah, I'm aware it might not work out that way, but if you could give me a few more hours, I'd really appreciate it."

"All right then. No problem."

"Great." Derek cast another look at his cell phone before he took a couple of bills out of his wallet. He didn't elaborate on the call. Jordan acknowledged it would be a while before she was fully in the loop again. But she was happy not to go back to the parking garage today.

Ellie never had the chance to finish her interview, as Jane used the distraction of the sirens to reach for Peterson's weapon. Gripping it tightly, she moved behind Ellie with surprising speed. Feeling the pressure of the gun's barrel against her back, Ellie winced. She had to think fast.

"All right, now get me out of here, or this won't end well," Jane threatened.

Peterson regarded her with utmost disdain.

"Don't be stupid. You hear those sirens? It's a lockdown. No one's getting out of here."

"Jane, give him the gun, please." Raising her hands slowly, Ellie was still convinced they could find a better way to resolve the situation. "Let's talk. I know you're scared, but this is not the way. You're making it worse for yourself."

She almost thought Peterson was rolling his eyes at her. He still stood in the same spot, behind the table where Jane had sat a few minutes ago, his expression impassive. Above all, Ellie was tired, strangely detached from what should be the most obvious emotion. However, she understood that all the events of the past minutes couldn't be unrelated.

"What do you think they're going to do, lock me up?"

"You were worried that if you talked, something might happen to you. Who's threatening you?"

"You can't do anything about this," Jane scoffed. "Why would you care?"

"I care about what happened to Martha, and Patty, and all women who might be in danger. That's why I'm here. But I can't help you if you do this."

"That's all right, sweetie. No one can help me."

Ellie didn't like the fatalistic tone in her voice. She wasn't sure if she could reach the woman. They had reached the last resort quickly.

"Please. Don't. I have a baby."

"So do I, sweetie. So do I."

Ellie braced herself. She caught the guard's gaze, angered by the almost bored expression on his face. It didn't look like she could rely on him much.

# Chapter Fourteen

As time went by neither Derek nor Pauline seemed much inclined to leave. As much as Jordan appreciated their presence, she was beginning to feel crowded in her own home. She wished she could go back to the quiet days she'd spent with Meri, before the incident, when the future was wide open.

She wasn't sure how to diplomatically ask them to leave either, when she owed both of them so much.

Ellie would be at work for a few more hours, but she sent a quick text anyway. M*iss you*. Likely, she wouldn't even have time to read it, being at the correctional facility all day. As a visitor, not going undercover for a period of time in which a lot could happen.

"Okay, you wanted to brainstorm or play with my kid?" she asked Derek who sat on the couch, entertaining an enthralled Meri.

"I'll be right with you," he said, clearly not in a hurry.

"Can I help you with anything else?" Pauline asked. "I could make you a coffee before I go."

"No, thanks, I think we had enough at the restaurant. Thank you so much for staying."

"Of course."

They hugged, and Pauline left.

"Okay, where were we?"

"You're sure it's okay we talk about this in front of her?"

"Come on. She doesn't understand the words."

"I read that babies pick up on vibes around them," he said, making her wonder when and why he had chosen that subject for reading material. Jordan didn't think it was the time, or her place, to raise any further questions. This was between him and Kate.

"They absolutely do, but the vibes are good. So, Boyd. A-student, has a group of close friends and loving parents. Late at night he walks away from his friends and—I don't buy it."

"We found no trace of another person. Nothing."

"So, we go back to an accident?"

"The banister was intact. No rain."

"We are running out of possible scenarios," she reminded him. "I'd like to see the scene, but honestly, I'll be ready for that once I've been cleared to go back. Call me if there's anything new?"

"What are you doing?"

Jordan thought Derek's reaction, when she picked up the remote control, was a bit extreme.

"I don't know, I'd like to watch the news? And maybe some *My Little Pony*. I know it's early for that, but Meri seems to like them."

"What are you having for dinner?"

"Really, stop it. You're extremely obvious, and no, you don't have to babysit me. Ellie and I are doing fine. Go back to work."

"We were working. I could watch Meri if you want to take a nap or something..."

"No, I don't want to take a nap. I'd like to watch some TV, and I think I'm able to do that by myself. Okay, what are you trying to hide from me?" It was meant to be a joke, but the more she thought about it, the more Jordan realized Derek's sudden abandonment of his plans for this afternoon might not be random. She'd just seen Pauline, and Meri was right next to them.

Ellie...Ellie was at work on the other side of town. Derek wasn't part of the task force, so he wouldn't know if something out of the ordinary had happened...

"Nothing. I just think you should take it easy as long as you can."

"That's why you keep wanting to discuss the case with me? Come on, I'm not stupid. What's going on?"

"Okay, but don't blame just me. The lieutenant thought it was a good idea."

"You're scaring me."

"Please keep in mind that we know next to nothing yet." He took the remote from her and turned on the news. Taking in the images and understanding what they meant, Jordan sat down, her hand going to her mouth.

"We don't know much," Derek repeated. "A fight broke out, a guard was injured, and apparently not all inmates are accounted for yet."

"There's no way this is random, with the task force doing their interviews today." Jordan picked up her cell phone, distantly aware that her hands were trembling. No message from Ellie. *Are you okay?* she texted. *Please call me when you can.*

"I want to go there. I want to speak to someone who's responsible."

"Everyone's doing what they can, and we'll get news whenever they have some, I promise. I know you want to be there, but it wouldn't do anyone any good. You have Meri to take care of, and I'll be here as long as you need me."

"God, I hate you," she said, not meaning it, but still wishing he'd given her any room to argue.

Derek understood her state of mind well enough not to be offended.

"That's okay. Look, we know how this will go down. They're going to end the lockdown and comb the building for that missing inmate. Ellie is probably stuck in some room with a couple of guards. She'll be fine."

"No, you don't understand." Jordan was aware that she was dangerously close to yelling, regardless of the fact that none of this was Derek's fault. "It's not fair! When do we get a break?"

"It'll be okay."

"So why did you spend all afternoon trying to keep me away from TV then?"

"I didn't want you to worry unless there was something to worry about."

Jordan shook her head. "You don't think that my wife being stuck in a women's prison, exact location unknown, is anything to worry about? Think again. What if this was Kate? I can't believe you. Don't do anything like that, ever again."

When he laid a hand on her shoulder, it was a small comfort, though by far not enough. She still wanted to scream.

⁂

Ellie had a small window of opportunity when Jane stepped to the side, and the sensation of the gun against her back disappeared momentarily. She cast a quick glance over her shoulder to realize Jane was focusing on Peterson now. The hand that held the gun trembled slightly, as if she was tiring.

Ellie used that moment to take the gun from her.

"No!" Jane cried, but Ellie was already at a safe distance, as safe as she could be in the confined space, and under the circumstances. It wasn't over yet.

"We'll protect you, I promise," she said, keeping her voice low. She could feel a drop of cold sweat sneaking down her spine, her emotional state not quite catching up with the physical one yet. As long as the three of them were cooped up in here together, she couldn't afford it.

Someone had facilitated bringing in the drugs that had killed Gaines and Webber, and it could have been someone like Peterson. It could have been him, for all she knew, but perhaps having a gun pressed against her back only a moment ago was making her paranoid.

Jane was crumbling in on herself, cowering in a corner.

Ellie took a deep breath, lightheadedness assailing her out of nowhere.

She'd had good reasons to decline the undercover assignment, and Jordan had given her more. Something neither of them had considered until now was that Ellie had her own demons lingering, and they were connected to confined spaces. She felt like her clothes were sticking to her skin, that the air inside the room was getting thinner. She couldn't go there, not now with the tension in the room still palpable as she handed Peterson the gun.

"You might want to keep that close."

"Watch out!" he yelled.

Ellie spun around, seeing Jane standing, raising her hands, but it was too late. Peterson had pulled the trigger.

Ellie didn't stand frozen in the horror she felt, instead she rushed to the woman's side to put pressure on the wound, blood seeping out from between her hands.

"Help me," she snapped. "What the hell did you do that for?"

"To save your damn life!" he seethed.

Ellie saw McAdams' eyes widen in terror as he stepped closer, and she made sure to stay between him and the woman.

"You're going to wear a hole in the floor. You're making me dizzy too," Derek complained. "Sit down, please."

"I hate that there's nothing we can do but wait." Irrationally, Jordan hated that her partner and boss had conspired to keep her out of the loop when she could have heard about the lockdown earlier. "Ellie didn't want to go. Because of me, because someone might have recognized her. But she really hates tight spaces."

Derek didn't comment. Seconds ticked by in silence.

"You know what I hate? Seeing someone's parents and having to tell them, sorry, we don't know yet if it was murder, suicide, or a freak accident. At the moment, the result is the same. They never get to talk to their son again."

"Yeah, that part sucks."

"I wasn't kidding, I wish you could come. You're better at this."

"Not true, but thanks anyway. I think Carroll might okay it, but for this time, I'll pass. I don't think Dr. Burns will have any objections, but I want to spend tomorrow with my family."

"I get it." A text message popped up on Derek's phone, and Jordan jumped to her feet.

"Relax. It's Kate."

"You should go. I'll be okay." When he didn't react, she added. "Ellie is Kate's best friend. She'll be worried too."

"She is. And she's coming over. You won't have to deal with anything tonight."

"You've got to be kidding me."

"After today, Ellie is not going to feel like cooking. And frankly, neither do any of us. Kate will be here in fifteen."

He probably hadn't expected her to pick up Meri and walk out of the room. Neither had she.

# Chapter Fifteen

"I want an officer in front of her room until we've figured this out. And don't let Peterson come anywhere near her."

Ellie spun around to find Cameron watching her. He'd spent the lockdown in an office with the female guard they'd met earlier, drinking coffee.

"You should clean up, Harding."

She looked down at herself, wincing at the dark stains on her jeans. She'd put her blouse in the garbage after using it to stench the flow of blood. Jane McAdams was alive, but she might still be in danger. There was a lot to unpack, but she didn't think she could do any of it today. Shivering, she wrapped her arms around herself. There was blood on her hands. What a messed-up day.

"I'd love a hot shower. At home."

"We can wrap up here. If you're ready, you can go. I'll see you tomorrow morning."

"Thanks."

"You did good in there," he said.

"I did what I had to do. See you tomorrow."

Another guard accompanied her to the waiting area for visitors where she finally got her cell phone back. *I'm okay. Coming home now.*

Then she put her jacket over her tank top and went outside where she called a cab. She wanted to sleep for eight hours straight, even though she was aware that it wasn't likely.

The driver had the radio on, and she recognized the voice of a local reporter, Jill Allen.

"Joy Anne Deane was charged with a hate crime earlier. She pled not guilty. Her trial is coming up…"

Ellie leaned forward in the seat, covering her face with her hands. Even though she'd washed them vigorously, she felt like she could still smell the blood. Too much blood.

They'd have to keep an eye on Peterson though. She didn't think he needed to shoot McAdams.

When Ellie let herself into the house, she stopped cold at the scene in front of her, Kate and Derek playing with Meri on the couch.

"Hey, that's my baby. You want one, you make your own," she said, for a moment not sure whether she was going to laugh or cry.

"Ellie!" Kate jumped to her feet and hugged her tightly. "I'm so glad you're okay."

"Me too." Over Kate's shoulder, Ellie caught Jordan's glance at her. "Those two invited themselves over for dinner, so I thought it was only fair if they paid for it. You want to come with me for a second?"

"Of course."

Ellie leaned down to kiss Meri's cheek before she followed Jordan out of the room and upstairs.

In their bedroom, Jordan pulled her close.

"Thank God you're home," she whispered.

With the danger past, Ellie was painfully aware of the exhaustion weighing down on her, on both of them.

"Honestly, I wish we could take a nap, but I need a shower, and we have guests. I...I'm sorry for scaring you." She didn't need to ask.

"You didn't do it on purpose. It's okay."

"I really need to take that shower now. Can we have Thai?"

"Absolutely." She waited. Ellie could guess the reason. She assumed Jordan was trying to assess her state of mind after the turbulent day, and if she should stay nearby in case its events caught up to Ellie.

"I'll be quick," she assured her. "I won't lie—I kind of want to fret about everything, but I guess it's a good thing we have friends who don't give us time for that."

Jordan kissed her softly.

"My thoughts exactly. I'll be downstairs. Thai it is."

❧

"Not to add to everything, but what do you make of Joy Anne pleading not guilty?" Kate asked. "That's crazy. It's all on video."

"She can't weasel her way out of that," Derek said. "A lot of people remember her badmouthing Ariel and the women who testified. The hate part is obvious every time she opens her mouth."

"And that's why we love having you over," Jordan said. "Dinner conversations are always lovely and uplifting."

"Says the woman who missed shop talk so much she wrote me three pages of notes."

Still exhausted, Ellie was nonetheless grateful for the presence of their friends. Especially on a day like this, they needed the notion that everything would be back to some kind of normal. Someday.

"Yeah, you weren't kidding. You really needed the help."

"I assume Carroll still wants me back on Monday," Ellie said. "In case you need more help."

"I can't wait. Maria and I have been bored without you guys."

The next challenge would be Jordan's appointment with Dr. Burns. A lot hinged on its outcome.

Ellie took a sip of her beer, intent on being grateful for the support of their friends, and for the lives they were able to lead, a path so different from that of Joy Anne Deane—or Jane McAdams. She hoped the latter would survive to tell her story.

"I'm grappling with this. I still don't sleep well, and I don't want to worry Ellie. I still hate going to the parking garage. But what I hate more is that my daughter is growing up in a world where women and girls are groomed to hate themselves so much they'll commit crimes like this. That about sums it up."

"Did you rehearse for this session?" Dr. Burns' question wasn't sarcastic at all. Her tone was still the same calm, interested one that Jordan found oddly soothing, and, at times, frustrating.

"A few weeks ago, I didn't think me coming back to work would even require one, yet, here we are."

"And we've been here before. I don't have to tell you that you're experiencing a normal reaction to an event that's everything but normal."

"I know I can do my job. It hasn't been easy, but I do have my coping strategies in place. I picked up a few things here."

Dr. Burns didn't need to know details about how exactly she'd been working on rebuilding her confidence. Ellie's unconditional acceptance and the way she expressed it had a lot to do with it. Jordan suppressed a smile as her thoughts wandered into a direction less appropriate for sharing.

"That's good to know. You seem very clear about where you want to go."

"Nothing gets you clarity like getting stabbed three times." They both winced, and the twinge of pain made it *very clear* no one was ready for jokes like that, least of all Jordan. "It's taking longer than I thought. That was...scary, but I don't know, maybe it had some benefits. I got to spend more time with my child."

"Is that the only reason?" Soothing was about to cross over into frustrating.

"What do you want me to say? It sucked. Yes, I could be home with her for a while longer, but I couldn't see her all the time I was in the hospital, and afterwards, I couldn't even hold her much right away. That other time, I needed to get back to work as soon as possible to save my sanity. It was the only place I felt safe. This...was close to home."

"I understand. And, experiences like those can pile up over time."

"I won't argue with that. But I'm treating myself better, too, these days. I want to do what I can to make the world a better place for Meri to grow up in. I still believe we can make a difference, that it matters." She shook her head with a laugh. "Now I sound like my wife. I guess that's what happens in marriage."

"It's not uncommon. And those are good ideas, anyway."

Yes, Ellie had good ideas. She was once again in danger going into inappropriate territory.

"To be frank, I hope they'll convince you to sign that form, because my partner has already planned out my week. But he's also Meri's Godfather, and he and his wife have helped us out a lot recently, so I'll forgive him."

Dr. Burns didn't comment on that, perhaps sensing that Jordan had more to say.

"That, and he's working on this new case. I know I can help him solve it."

⁂

As they worked together with the prison's director and staff to untangle the events that had led to the death of two inmates, and a knife fight that caused the lockdown, Ellie couldn't be happier that her time with the task force was coming to an end. She was aware that not every single one of her colleagues had appreciated her quick rise through the ranks. She couldn't change their minds, and she didn't waste her time trying.

Together with Cameron, she watched while two of her colleagues in the task force interrogated Peterson. He couldn't wait to implicate his supervisors.

"Crystal Sherman came out of hiding as well when she realized we caught him," Cameron explained. "She'll testify."

"That's a good thing."

"It is," he agreed. "I'm sorry you had to do this work under such difficult circumstances."

Ellie was aware he probably didn't mean the lockdown and subsequent events.

"Thank you," she said.

After Peterson had finished his statement, she went to see Jane McAdams in the hospital, she couldn't help flash back to the scene that led to the shooting. Ellie regretted putting that gun into Peterson's hands. When she told her, Jane made a dismissive gesture.

"To be fair, you didn't have that many options either."

"He could have killed you. I'm so sorry."

"But I hear that then you saved my life, so that counts for something, I guess. Is it really over?"

Ellie took a seat in the chair. "Peterson is turning on some higher-ups that were involved. There will be more internal investigations, but he did run his operation under their eyes, getting the drugs inside. Patty overdosed. Kayla was a witness. We found Crystal Sherman too."

Could she have figured all of this out if she'd gone undercover, with no one getting hurt?

Jane took a deep breath, before she confessed, "We had to do something while you were there. That was our last chance. We knew that a fight would lead to a lockdown, and we hoped it would keep you on the inside long enough to figure out what was going on. No hard feelings?"

"Just stay under the radar. I hear your contribution could be helpful when it comes to your release."

"Detective Ellie Harding." McAdams smiled, if a bit pained, meds likely wearing off. "I'll remember that name."

"Well, I don't want to hear your name at work again. I hope you get well soon."

She couldn't believe she was going to write her final report. It seemed like an eternity, but she'd finally return to her own desk.

# Chapter Sixteen

J ordan stood over the parking spot, arms crossed over her chest. She wasn't feeling much of anything. There was no visual reminder of the incident, the blood cleaned off the concrete after all evidence of the crime scene had been collected and catalogued. Truth be told, she might have hoped for one final cathartic event that would free her forever from the memory, though she knew from experience it didn't work that way.

"I guess this is all the confronting you can do," Derek said behind her, and she almost didn't flinch. They were going to see Boyd's friends at their college, a car ride about an hour out of town. "You're ready?"

"Yeah." He was right. There was nothing else here for her to do. She'd see Joy Anne Deane at the trial, a confused and hateful twenty-something she felt mostly pity for. The demons were elsewhere, lingering, but she had never been better equipped to fight them off.

"Let's go."

As of today, Jordan was officially back at work, and she had ideas on how to move the case forward.

She had read and memorized Derek's report on the interview with the parents. Jordan was still convinced that the friends had more to say.

Brent Ellis, one of the two friends on the camping trip, was in class. The other, Jason Shelby, sat down with them in a coffee shop. He had texted Brent to join them as soon as he left class.

"I don't know what else to tell you," he said. "It's horrible. We keep asking ourselves why this happened when it did."

"Oliver's parents told us he had been battling depression."

Jason shrugged. "We knew about that, but he seemed fine...He went to therapy a few years ago, but I didn't think it was something he had to take meds for."

"Okay. Who suggested the trip?"

"It was something we'd been planning for a while. Both Oliver and Brent are from around here, so they knew places...and also a few bars." He blushed. Jordan remembered that he was the only one in the group under twenty-one, but she was willing to let that go for a moment.

"Mixing alcohol and hiking? Who thought that was a good idea?"

"Oliver didn't drink. Brent and I just had a few beers, and then we went back to the camp." He seemed distraught, but that wasn't unexpected, given what had happened next.

"When did you realize he was missing?"

"The next morning. We went to look for him, and..." Jason paled, looking as if he might throw up. "God, I wish I could help you, but I have no idea. He went up there by himself and jumped. There is no other explanation."

"You wanted to talk to me?"

Brent Ellis had joined them, but he made no move to sit down.

"Yes. Please, sit," Derek instructed. "You'd like a coffee?"

"No thanks, I'm good. I don't have a lot of time."

Jordan hadn't missed the look he and Jason exchanged. Contrary to his friend, Brent acted cool and wary.

"Jason already told us a bit about what you think happened on the trip."

"What we think? I'm sure Oliver's parents told you about his depressive phases. He saw a therapist at some point. It's pretty obvious what happened, don't you think?"

"You went on a trip, had fun, had a few beers...what changed?"

"How would I know? He must have planned this before."

"Come on, man," Jason interjected. "They are trying to help."

"Really? Then please, wrap this up and let us move on. This is hard enough without being reminded every damn day."

"I know this is hard," Jordan said, softening her tone. "But don't you think it's important to figure out what exactly happened?"

Brent gave her a hard stare. "You're Homicide detectives, right? You think Jason or I murdered him? He was our best friend!"

"No, I don't think that. But you might have observed something that could help us figure out what happened."

"Oliver killed himself. We might never know why. Now let him rest in peace. If that's all, Detectives? I have to get back to my class."

Even Jason seemed surprised by his reaction. "I have to go, too," he said. "Thanks for the coffee. "I hope you can find out what happened."

"You and me both," Derek mumbled when the two young men were out of earshot. "Now what? We go home?"

"Not yet. We could have lunch here, give them a bit of time."

"Go on," he said, intrigued.

"I have a feeling Brent has a bit more to tell. Let's give him the opportunity to do so."

"You don't think he had something to do with this? You know, there were no traces of another person where Boyd jumped...or fell."

"I know, but I think he might have some information to help us wrap this up. Everyone says Boyd was doing well. His grades were excellent, he had good friends...If he jumped, something triggered him into doing it. Something that might have happened before or during the trip."

"He didn't have a girlfriend," Derek said.

"Or boyfriend."

"Or boyfriend, but that's beside the point, I think. He was focusing on his studies."

"Maybe it was a secret relationship that ended. Someone who had something to lose."

"A teacher?" Derek frowned. "Now you're far into the obscure."

"Low blood sugar," Jordan said. "Let's get something other than coffee and let me talk to Brent again. I know there's something there."

"Okay, but after that we're going back."

"Sure."

For a moment, Jordan thought Brent might bolt when he saw her standing next to the door of his dorm. He resorted to glaring at her.

"You didn't believe me?"

"I don't think you lied to us. You might have left out some information."

"Like what?"

"Let's walk a few steps?" she suggested.

"Do I have a choice?"

He didn't resist any longer though, and they went along the path leading to the park behind the building.

"I don't understand why you even came back here. We told the other officers everything we knew already. You want more of a story? It's not even relevant."

"Let me be the judge of that. You went on the trip, arrived in town and hit a few bars. All of you were single?"

His expression was somewhere between resigned and angry, as if he couldn't decide what to feel. "Jason has a girlfriend, but we weren't there to hook up anyway. Or that's what I thought. I'm not sure what to think anymore." He looked straight ahead as he spoke. "All right, this is what happened. A few weeks ago, at a party, we got pretty drunk. Oliver kissed me. I told him I'm not gay. Now he's dead. There's your story, Detective."

"I'm so sorry." Jordan had imagined that the truth would be more complex than the reports revealed. It turned out to be a whole lot more tragic.

"Well, sorry doesn't change anything. I mean, I wasn't an ass about it, I just said no. I'll always wonder if he did it because—"

"I'm sure that's not the case. Did you know if he was bullied?"

"I didn't even think anyone knew. Except the guy he was making out with that night at the *D&T*." He shook his head. "This is all so messed up."

"That guy, do you remember what he looked like?"

"Sure, but why does it matter? We went back to the camp. We had a hike planned for the next day. Instead, Oliver decided to go out to that viewpoint and jump."

"I'd like to talk to that man anyway. Thank you for telling the whole story. And don't blame yourself. I'm sure Oliver understood you didn't reject him as a person."

But what had been on his mind that night? And why were witnesses always this selective about the information they cared to share? That guy could be anywhere by now.

"You know what the worst thing is?" Brent said. "I wasn't even all that sure. Maybe I wanted him to kiss me."

Jordan didn't envy him.

"I know this is hard, but it still wouldn't make anything your fault. You'll figure it out. Talk to someone."

"Thank you," he said after a moment of hesitation. "I'm sorry I didn't tell you earlier."

"It's not easy. But we will find answers. I need you to come in tomorrow for a facial composite."

"Of course."

When she went back to find where Derek had parked on the curb and sat in the car, Jordan couldn't suppress the sigh.

"Thank God for not being that age anymore."

She shared what new information she had learned.

Derek looked doubtful. "This is all interesting, but I'm not sure if finding that guy will help him with any of those questions."

"Maybe not, but what if Oliver had other secrets? I'm not sure this is even all."

"I hate suicide cases," he said emphatically.

"Yeah. Me too."

"Hey. You're early," Dan greeted them when they walked through the door of the *D&T*, named after its two owners, Dan and Teddy. Jordan and Ellie had come on a regular basis, and since it was close to the precinct, some of their colleagues had adopted the habit. Now that Jack had opened the *SEVEN*, they hadn't made it in a while. "How are you doing? What can I bring you?"

"I'm afraid we're here on official business today." Jordan wasn't sure how much attention he had paid to recent news or the part where she'd been in them. To her relief, Dan didn't mention it at all.

"Is this about Jerry? I hoped he'd press charges, but I wasn't sure...Wait a minute. What happened to him?"

"I'm pretty sure we aren't talking about the same thing," Jordan said. "But you can tell me, and we can follow up on it if you want. I have a college kid who jumped or fell to his death. The night before it happened, he was here with a couple of buddies. One of them told us he was making out with someone. We're trying to find that guy."

"You think he had something to do with it?"

"We don't know yet. We're following all leads."

"I hate to say it, but we might be talking about the same thing. Jerry got beaten up that night. He didn't see who did it, but what are the odds? The same night one of them kills himself?"

"Do you remember them at all?" Jordan asked.

"I remember a group of twenty-somethings that came in, thinking they might be trouble. But they had a few drinks and left. I didn't have time to pay much attention that night. Jerry came by the next day and told me what happened."

"Okay. We need to talk to him."

"I was afraid you'd say that." He sighed. "He said getting the police involved might be more trouble than leaving it alone."

"Hey, Dan. You know me. I come here with my *wife*. You really think we'd try to frame him for anything?"

"No, of course not. Not you. I'm sorry. We're a bit on edge since...Well, you know. A couple of years actually. Here's his number. And for the record, I'm glad that Deane woman is behind bars. They'll never give up, will they?"

"Neither will we. Thank you, Dan."

# Chapter
# Seventeen

J erry was on his way home from work, and he asked if they could come to his apartment.

On the way, Jordan received a text message from Ellie, asking her to come to the *SEVEN* tonight for dinner. She started to respond, then changed her mind and called instead. "Things are moving, but I think we could be there in an hour or so."

"Sounds good," Ellie said. "I asked Kate to come over too. We'll see you there."

Ten minutes later, Jordan and Derek rode up the elevator to Jerry Morgan's apartment. When he opened the door to them, they could still see faint traces of bruises in his face.

"I know Dan sent you, and I appreciate it, but I don't really want to press charges. Too much stress, not worth the outcome. No offense."

"Mr. Morgan, I'm Detective Carpenter, this is Detective Henderson."

"Wait. You're the cop who got stabbed by that nutcase."

Jordan winced. She didn't let the unexpected statement get her off track.

"It's your decision whether to press charges, but perhaps we can help each other. You recognize him?" She showed him a picture of Oliver Boyd.

"Yes. I met him that night. Is it true that he killed himself? What a lousy world we live in."

"It's what we're trying to find out. Dan thought his friends might have given you trouble?"

"Can't say for sure. It was dark, I didn't see whoever did it, coming. But one of his buddies was definitely not amused, kept giving me the evil eye. I think he didn't realize right away they were in a gay bar."

"Did Oliver tell you anything about himself? Something that might explain..."

Jerry shook his head. "After that jerk jumped me, someone called an ambulance, and I spent the night in the hospital. Took a couple of days sick leave afterwards. I didn't even realize Oliver was the guy I met that night until I saw his picture. I was shocked. I mean I didn't get to know him that well, but he didn't seem depressed at all. Very much at ease, with himself, in the place."

It started to feel like she and Derek were going around in circles with this case—or Oliver's friends weren't as innocent as they tried to convey.

"It's only going to get worse, right?" he asked. "You must see it too. We thought those Prophets were whacko, but now everyone feels like they have the right to be an asshole."

"Do you want to press charges?"

"As I said, I don't see the point. That lady from the cult, I heard she won't be going to prison, but some psychiatric facility instead. And you're a cop."

"I don't know where you heard that. She'll go to trial first. How did you and Oliver part?"

If that was abrupt, Jordan didn't care. She wasn't here to talk about herself, or how Joy Anne Deane's actions might fit into a larger story.

"I gave him my number after we left the hotel, but he never called. Obviously, I didn't think much of it. We had a good time that night...but what are the odds that this happens the same night?"

"Wait a minute, Jerry. What hotel?"

He looked confused. "You didn't know that? He was going to join his friends later at the campground. I guess he never made it there."

"When exactly did you leave the hotel?"

As he described the timeline of that evening, Jordan could identify a few pieces that didn't fit the picture Jason and Brent had painted. Both had confirmed that all of them had left the *D&T* together.

Jerry's version of the story differed in interesting ways.

"It's all too convenient," she told Derek once they were in the car, on the way to the *SEVEN*. "He's right. Him getting attacked the same night, that's no coincidence. Those guys didn't tell us the whole truth."

"I don't know. Maybe it is coincidence."

"What's that supposed to mean?"

"As for Oliver Boyd, it's tragic. We both know that even if no one else saw the signs, it doesn't mean he wasn't depressed. It doesn't have to be some big secret. Ellis might have been worried about his own secret coming out. I don't think it has to do with Boyd's death though. And Morgan's not wrong to say the world is going to hell in a hand basket. Don't be mad, but I think you're a little too close to all of this."

"Wow."

"I don't think I'm wrong."

"You are. This has nothing to do with me."

"You think there's some anti-gay predator out there who doesn't leave any trace? A ghost?"

"We don't close a case until we have a logical conclusion. This one keeps defying logic."

"I'm sorry but we'll have to close it soon. The kid killed himself. It's terrible, but there's only so much we can do."

"Maybe you're right." Jordan wasn't entirely convinced, but she didn't feel like arguing any longer, and truth be told, she didn't have any compelling points at the moment. "Let's go eat."

Jack and Pauline had set up in the private room, buffet-style, while only a few feet away, the usual bar business continued. The noise from the main room was faint enough for Meri to sleep soundly in her car seat next to her. The scattered parts of the case that didn't seem to fit together still bothered her. She might have to let it go.

⁂

Later that night, Ellie was studying something on her tablet when Jordan came out of the shower clad in a towel.

Ellie was wearing a tank top and shorts, frowning at something she was reading before she looked up at Jordan and smiled.

"You were saying?"

"What? I wasn't saying anything."

"Oh, you were," Ellie insisted. "If you wanted to distract me from this, it's working."

Not all of Jordan's fears had come true in the course of becoming a mother. She had been, and was still sometimes battling anxiety, worrying that being bad at this was in her genes. She'd wanted Meri more than anything. At the same time, she'd wondered if this new dynamic would change her relationship with Ellie, and that was before the incident.

118

She had to learn that no matter how many books and blogs she'd read, no matter how much good advice she'd received from her parents and friends, there were still moments when they figured things out as they went along. Meri would always be safe with them.

And her relationship with Ellie had grown stronger, closer.

"Good," Jordan said, and Ellie put the tablet aside before she leaned over and gave the towel a firm tug.

With Joy Anne Deane's trial coming up, there was a lot of speculation in the media, from major outlets to private LGBT related blogs. No one would know for sure, but there was an air of resignation, people wondering if Deane would pay accordingly for her crime. Already, there was a crowd-funding campaign for her legal bills.

Jordan slept, blissfully relaxed, while Ellie wondered how people could have changed their minds on the Prophets so quickly. Or maybe they hadn't, maybe there were some willing to forgive a group that had harbored a murderer, as long as they hated women and gay people enough. What a world to bring a child into, even if they tried everything to protect her and help her become a strong woman who would know her worth.

What would be the right way to deal with criminals like Joy Anne? Ellie thought that Valerie Esposito was right to charge her with a hate crime, because that's what it was. If she went to prison, she might successfully adopt the role of a martyr. Would psychiatric intervention make her understand that she and the Prophets were wrong, and had always been wrong? Ellie doubted that too, but whatever made the world safer from her, and people like her, would be a start.

The adults in the house weren't the only ones to have night-mares stemming from recent events, as it seemed. Meri's high-pitched scream woke them both at close to four a.m. Jordan and Ellie were by her bed within seconds.

A quick examination revealed nothing out of the ordinary, just the necessity for a fresh diaper and some human contact.

"How's it going with your case?" Ellie asked as she put away supplies. "I heard the parents on the radio."

Rocking Meri back to sleep, Jordan shrugged. "I'd like for it to go faster, but some new questions came up. I feel for the parents, but as long as there's doubt..."

"Yeah. Let me know if you need help on anything."

"I will." Jordan kissed the top of Meri's head. "Someone's ready to get back to sleep. What about you? Would you like some breakfast and brainstorming, like the old days?"

"At four a.m.? I'm not so sure. I think we have a shot at two more hours."

"That sounds like a plan." Jordan carefully laid Meri back into her bed, studying her.

"She's fine."

"I know. Just a little stressed, like the rest of us."

Ellie let the statement stand, acknowledging that while the worst was behind them, they all still felt the ripples of a trau-matic time.

# Chapter Eighteen

"Where are we on pending cases? Harding, the task force is all wrapped up?"

"Yes. My report is ready. Cameron is finishing up with Crystal Sherman, the guard who went missing."

"Sounds good. Carpenter, Henderson, you're ready to close the file on Boyd?"

"Not yet, sir. There's been a new development," Jordan said. "I'm starting to doubt the suicide theory."

Derek looked unsure, though he didn't contradict her.

Even though the tone was professional and even a tad urgent, Ellie had a hard time suppressing a smile. It might be selfish, but she was so happy to be back with this group, including some of her closest friends and colleagues, most importantly, including Jordan.

"Please do me a favor and find something to back up your doubts soon."

"Yes sir."

He made the round for a quick update, ending with A.D.A. Esposito who sat next to him.

"Good morning," she said. "I'm sure you all know why I'm here. I'm going to need to sit down with each of you over the next few days."

"Did anything change?" Derek asked, suspicious. "There's no way she's going to a hospital instead of prison? Come on, we all know the difference."

Jordan didn't comment, but Ellie recognized the flash of irritation in her expression, and everything behind it. Yes, they wanted to put all of it behind them, but first, they'd have to make it through the trial. Ellie didn't doubt that Joy Anne Deane had a few homophobic rants saved for the occasion, no matter what the lawyer told her to say. On the bright side, that might make a good argument for showing her as the criminal she was. Intent. Ellie had seen the damage she'd done up close. She felt a familiar anger rise within her.

"I'll talk with each of you, but remember, when you're on the stand, don't let them twist your words. Stick to the facts."

"Don't worry. This is not our first time," Maria Doss reminded her.

"I'm aware, but there's a lot at stake here. Let's just get through this. She is going to make our case, no matter what anyone says, or how much money she gets from her crowd-funding campaign."

"So that part wasn't a joke?" Derek shook his head. "People never cease to disgust."

"Are we all done here?" Jordan asked. "I have some calls to make."

"Just one more thing. Ellie, they might call you to clarify what exactly happened during your conversation with her."

Great. Ellie suppressed a curse, aware that Jordan had just sat up straighter. She meant to tell her about her lapse in reason, but there had been so much on her mind. After Lieutenant Carroll and IA had considered the case closed—not that there was much of a case—she'd simply forgotten.

"I talked to IA already," she said. Jordan gave her a quizzical look.

"So did I," Carroll confirmed. "And there's nothing to worry about here. If anything, it puts Ms. Deane's motive on display even more. Okay folks, that's all, back to work. Make sure you make time for A.D.A. Esposito."

Everyone got to their feet.

"Ellie, can I talk to you for a moment?" So, there was no way to avoid that conversation any longer. Just as well. She never meant to keep her misstep a secret.

"Sure."

They walked to the break room where a couple of officers were having a coffee.

"Guys, could you give us a minute?" Jordan's tone didn't leave much room for negotiation, and they both left.

"I'm a bit uncomfortable being once again the last to know. Tell me what happened."

"I messed up. I'm not proud of it, but as you saw, IA and the lieutenant already read me the riot act, and it will be fine."

"What did you do?" Against all odds, Jordan sounded a bit amused—and proud. But perhaps Ellie was imagining that.

"I swear I wanted to tell you, but in the grand scheme I didn't think it was that important. All I wanted was for you to get better."

"I understand. So?"

Ellie wondered if she could relate the story without cringing if she talked fast. It was worth a try. "So, I went into the room while she was here for interrogation, and I told her she was jealous because she had no idea what love is. She spit at me. Not a metaphor. But that's about the gist of it."

"Okay." Jordan turned to the vending machine and purchased a couple of coffees and a chocolate bar.

"Okay? That's all?" Ellie asked incredulously.

She wasn't prepared for Jordan to pull her into a tight embrace after putting her purchases on the table.

"I wanted to tell you."

"I know. She won't be able to twist that into something different. It would have been better to stay away…"

"Don't I know it." Ellie sighed.

"…but I can't say for sure I wouldn't have done the same thing."

"You're not mad at me?"

"Why would I be mad? You only told the truth. And if it comes to that, you'll do the same in court. Why should anyone believe a woman who was complicit in the abuse of children, over you?"

Ellie let the comfort of the embrace wash over her for a moment.

"Thank you. For the hug and the coffee. I guess we both have to get back to work now. Half of that chocolate bar is mine, right?"

"Um, it wasn't supposed to be…"

The door opened, and Maria Doss walked in, halting in her tracks. "Can I come in, or are you still having a moment?"

"Be nice," Jordan advised before she picked up her coffee and snatched the bar from the table. "This is why Derek never brings you coffee."

"Talk about nice," Ellie said out loud. "I really needed that chocolate."

"You guys okay?" Maria, now serious, asked.

"Oh yes, better than that."

"Good. You know Val is going to get the job done."

"Yes. I know."

Jordan called both Brent Ellis and Jason Shelby to come in, preferably the same day. As predicted, Jason agreed right away while Brent was suspicious.

"What else is there? Didn't you find the guy?"

She had decided not to confront him about the holes in his story over the phone.

"We only have a few more things to confirm. We're grateful for your cooperation."

"Not like we can do anything about it," he muttered. "I'll catch a ride with Jason."

"Thank you, Brent. See you later."

Being at the center of the Deane case, Valerie would have her testify as well. Jordan remembered what Jerry and Dan had said, about the increase in hate crimes being a sign of the times. But could these instances be related? Did the Prophets of Better Days make an effort to rebuild, or did garden variety bigots simply feel emboldened?

And how did Oliver Boyd fit into this? It bothered her that after everything she'd seen and read, after all the conversations with people closest to him and a casual hook-up, she still couldn't get a clear image.

Was she too distracted? By what happened to her, by her longing to be home with Meri again? She shook her head. No. Something was odd about this case, and she felt they were nowhere near uncovering why Boyd had died.

Maybe Derek was right, and she was too close to this one, but the questions remained.

"Would you like something to drink? Water, a soda?" Jordan asked a brooding Brent Ellis. Derek had gone to another room with Jason.

"No, thanks. I need to get back home as soon as possible. I have to study."

"Okay." She sat across from him. Brent was holding her gaze, though he looked uncomfortable. Not that it had to mean anything. For all she knew, he was grieving a friend who could have been something else. "I went over your statement, and Jason's, and I noticed something. You said Oliver went back to the campsite with you, and he disappeared the same night."

"That's what we said. A million times."

"Right. My problem is...Oliver's date—" He scoffed at her choice of a term. "He said Oliver went to a hotel with him, and that he was planning to join you after. Both can't be true. Brent?"

"What the hell do you want me to say? It makes no difference, does it? He's dead."

"True, but it might make a big difference in how he died. Someone might have followed him, saw him leave that hotel. The other man was beaten up the same night. Some of those parts don't fit together, don't you think?"

"I don't know what to think. I don't know anything about that other guy, and I sure as hell didn't beat up anyone. Can I have a coffee?"

"Are you going to tell me what really happened?"

Resigned, he nodded, and Jordan got up to get the coffee. On her way, she knocked on the door of the room where Derek was sitting at a table with Jason. Derek got up to join her outside.

"I doubt he knows much of anything," he said with a nod to the young man behind the glass. "How's it going on your end?"

"I think he's about to tell me something, but I agree, I don't think you'll learn much from Jason. I'll get back to you in a bit."

"All right."

When she stepped back into the room with the coffee, Brent had leaned forward, his head in his hands. Jordan closed the door behind her softly and put the hot beverage in front of him.

"Let's talk."

"Okay, so we left without him. I didn't think it mattered. Depression is like that, you can't always tell."

"I'm aware. But why not tell the truth? You and Jason decided on this version together?"

"Yes. And I swear I don't know what happened to the other guy. We just thought it was better...I don't know anymore."

"Do you know if Oliver met or talked to someone else that night?"

"What the hell are you insinuating?"

"Nothing. If we close the case, I want to make sure we got the whole story."

"Well, that's all the story I can tell you. If there were no signs of violence, or of an accident, then that's what it must be, right? Suicide?"

Jordan had to admit Ellis' revelations weren't quite as extensive as she'd hoped.

"Thank you for coming in. I think Jason's interview is finished as well."

# Chapter Nineteen

"Look, I want to get home fast, too, but without getting pulled over, if possible," Ellie commented when they were on their way.

With a sigh, Jordan slowed down the car. "You're right. I'm sorry."

"You did everything you could. And for what it's worth, I think it mattered to Brent Ellis that he could tell the truth, that there were people who wouldn't judge him or Oliver." Ellie leaned back in her seat. "Wow. That's got to be rough. Coming out is a challenge even when the stars align, and they certainly didn't in this case."

"His parents were okay. He was rejected by his best friend, which had to hurt, but...I still don't buy it. The doctor confirmed that he took meds only for a short time, and that was years ago."

"It could come back. Being away at college, it's a difficult time for many."

"Why on that trip? Why that way?"

"We might never know," Ellie reminded her gently.

"Yeah. I think I need to do a hiking trip before I can close that file. Are you game?"

⁂

Early the next morning, Kate arrived to watch Meri, before Jordan and Ellie drove to the *D&T*. From there they followed the path to the place where Boyd and his friend had camped. They parked the car at a restaurant welcoming hikers and continued on foot.

"Isn't it strange?" Ellie wondered out loud. "I mean they said he wasn't drinking, so he could drive out here. Maybe someone took him. He went all the way to the camp—at night?"

"I don't know," Jordan said. "He might have gone straight to the cliff." She was aware of Ellie watching her closely. "Stop that. If I can work, I can do a little hike."

The only other time she'd seen the scene, a park ranger had driven her and Derek in his vehicle which got them closer. Today, they wanted to take the same route Oliver had taken. The three men's campsite had been about twenty minutes from the check-in point. From there, they had twenty to thirty minutes more to get to the cliff.

"I didn't say anything," Ellie defended herself. "But you tell me if you need a break."

"Don't worry, I will."

It didn't surprise either of them that there had been no tracks. Wind and rain had taken care of that, though the weather hadn't been bad enough to justify the theory of an accident. Ahead of the drop, signs warned the visitors of danger. The railing was high enough that no one would stumble and fall accidentally, even at night. But if Oliver Boyd was as responsible as his friends said he was, why would he come up here at that time?

Jordan didn't mention anything, even when her body reminded her of recent events. By the time they had reached the railing built to protect campers that wanted to enjoy the view, she was glad she had something to lean on.

Ellie once more, silently, produced a water bottle from the backpack she'd brought.

"Thanks."

"What are you thinking?"

"I'm still thinking, him, Jerry, it's all too much of a coincidence, but it doesn't look like we're going to find anything here. If anyone did this to him, they're a ghost."

Ellie shuddered. "I didn't know you believed in ghosts."

"I don't. I believe we overlooked something, and it's driving me mad."

"You've been at this longer than I have. Do you think everyone's right? That Joy Anne won't get to plead insanity?"

It wasn't a subject Jordan had expected, and she didn't care to deepen it. But it was obvious Ellie worried about it.

"I don't know," she said honestly. "Most people want to see somebody who attacked a cop, go away for a long time. The Prophets, especially the women who took part in all this crap, are a special case."

"There's no medication against bigotry."

"No, there isn't." Jordan took a look around, imagining Oliver Boyd coming up here at night...ending his life? A faint sensation made her spin around, but Ellie was still standing a couple of feet away, hands in the pockets of her jeans.

Ghosts indeed. She might have overestimated herself on various levels.

"Let's go home," she said. "There's nothing here."

# Chapter Twenty

T he week leading up to the trial turned out to be more difficult than expected. Jordan wasn't surprised when the nightmares returned, of the parking garage, of a predator's basement, the two mingling on occasion. She was sorry to rob Ellie of her sleep, seeing in her haunted gaze how much she understood about the subconscious struggling with the reality of a close call.

But no matter her own nightmares, Ellie was always there, steadfast, holding her close.

"Come on," she said after a while, and they got up and tiptoed close to Meri's bed.

"You think that one day, she might find it creepy that we got up in the middle of the night to watch her sleep?"

She could see Ellie tear up. "I wasn't serious, you know."

"I know. I think she'll be happy to know she reminded us that we're not surrounded by evil and ignorance."

"There is that. Hell, I don't know why. Valerie knows her job. I'm not worried."

"Neither am I."

Ellie might have promised too much, but she was too grateful for the relative equilibrium they'd found in the aftermath of the brutal disruption of her lives. She didn't want to burden Jordan, or herself, with constant thoughts about how most ignorant dangerous individuals lived their lives day after day, hurting others, without anyone ever being able to hold them accountable.

She hoped that Joy Anne's case might shine a spotlight on where ideology could lead, but that might be a tad too optimistic.

In the courtroom, she noticed with grim satisfaction the many friends and colleagues behind her when she turned around in her seat. At least this meant it would soon be over, and they could get on with their lives for real.

The only person with Joy Anne was the lawyer who looked like she'd recently graduated law school. Looks could be deceiving. Their research had shown that she had taken on high profile cases before. She was good, but they had a lot on their side of the scale. It had to be enough for justice. For Ariel, the other women, and most of all for Jordan.

Ellie had seen the video from the security camera before, the images burned into her mind. She could easily understand why Jordan was drawn into the horrors of the past and the memory of another video, directed by another violent psychopath.

The graphic footage, Derek's and Maria's testimony, she could tell that the members of the jury were shocked and moved by their accounts. They were both seasoned cops, and they answered Valerie's questions calmly and to the point.

The lawyer had no questions for Derek, but she rose to question Maria.

"You described earlier how you arrested Ms. Deane, near the house where her children's foster family lived."

"Yes. I think everyone remembers, since I did it only a few minutes ago."

"Detective," the judge warned.

"I'm sorry. Like I said before, we found her in the park across the street, the bloody knife still on her."

Ellie saw more than one of the jurors wince. She was ready to flee, but of course she wouldn't. None of their friends and colleagues would, as disturbing the images shown and evoked were.

"Were you aware who Joy Anne Deane was at the time?"

Even in two-and-a-half inch heels, the woman couldn't be more than 5'3. She sounded painfully young. Ellie wondered if that was part of the strategy, to appear non-threatening to the jury, and, by proxy, cast a new light on her client.

"When I arrested her? Oh yes, I was aware. All of us worked on the Prophets' case that led to numerous arrests of members of the cult. Ms. Deane was a witness at the time."

"I assume you have arrested many suspects. Would you say it's the usual that they still carry the weapon with them?"

"It happens, if we're lucky," Maria said, unfazed.

"But not very often?"

"No. But it happens."

"What do you think is the reason for someone to do that?"

"Objection," Valerie interjected. "Relevance."

"I'll allow it," the judge announced, "but please, Counselor, get to the point."

"Yes, thank you, Your Honor. Let me rephrase. Do you think Ms. Deane was able to understand that what she'd done was wrong by our standards even if she didn't think to get rid of the weapon?"

"Objection! Detective Doss isn't a psychiatrist nor a mind reader."

"I'll withdraw." She sent a quick wry smile to her opponent. "My point is simple. My client is accused of a hate crime, but we simply don't have enough context for that. A.D.A. Esposito correctly pointed out that you're no psychiatrist, Detective Doss. Could it be that you missed something that day?"

"Like what? You saw the video, you saw what she did. We identified her, arrested her with the weapon still on her, and she confessed. In fact, Ms. Deane was happy to give us details regarding her motivation."

"She missed her children." As if she'd had eyes in the back of her head to see the stormy look on Valerie's face, the woman switched gears and turned her statement into a question. "That's what she told you, isn't it?"

"Yes. She also told me that no child should be with gay parents, and that they are an abomination."

"Thank you, Detective, I would like to—"

"Wait, you didn't want to hear more? She said that she hated the thought of Ariel Deane, or any of her own kids, growing up with homosexuals."

"Detective."

"...that it would be better for all of them if they were still on the compound with their murdering family members."

"Detective, that's enough." This time, it wasn't the lawyer but the judge who had spoken. "The jury will disregard."

"I'm sorry, Your Honor. The counselor wanted some context as to why this is considered a hate crime. My answer is that every word Ms. Joy Anne Deane has said to any of us, or in a courtroom, points to that. So no, I didn't miss anything, and neither did any of my colleagues that day."

"May we approach?" Valerie almost spoke over Maria's last word. The judge waved her and Joy Anne's attorney closer. Ellie couldn't hear the exchange, but after it was over, questions and answers seemed shorter and more focused.

Regardless, she'd felt every word that Maria had said, and she hoped the jurors would too.

Ellie studied Joy Anne Deane, once more wondering what it would take to break through to her. Or to the many others who didn't commit crimes but had similar thoughts about family and marriage. She and her family, and the people who loved them, would persist. One way or another.

⸙

"That didn't go so badly," Ellie said when they could finally get to bed that day. Jordan had not been present yet since Valerie was going to call her on the stand.

"Yeah," she agreed after a yawn. "Sounds like it."

"Maria got warned a couple of times. Not that I don't understand."

"At least Val wasn't mad at me this time." Jordan had testified in the previous case against the Prophets of Better Days, and she could sympathize with Maria Doss. "It would be hard to make Joy Anne look sympathetic. I hate to think what she would have put her children through—and what she already did to Ariel and others."

"I love you so much. I don't what I would have done if—" Truth be told, Deane's children and even Ariel had been second on Ellie's mind, even though Jordan had a point.

"Shh. Don't think about it. We're okay."

"I know. I'm glad everyone is coming out to support you."

"Me too. But we should try to get some sleep," Jordan said, reminding Ellie that she valued and needed her space—even from well-meaning colleagues and friends.

"I know everyone has helped out a lot, and we owe them, but sometime soon, we should have a nice quiet weekend, just the three of us."

"I'd love that." The longing tone in Jordan's voice spoke volumes.

"After this is done. For sure."

"I can't wait."

# Chapter Twenty-One

The next day, the morning sky was dark and grey with low rain clouds. Meri was fussy, not amused that both of her mothers were getting ready to leave early once again.

"Don't worry," Pauline said. "She's just not a morning person."

Jordan appreciated her attempt at injecting some humor into a tense situation.

"Things will be a bit less rushed once this is over. They should wrap up the trial soon enough."

"I hope so," Pauline said. "You've earned a break."

"So have you and Jack. You've spent a lot of time here while still running the bar."

"We were glad to do it. And many of our patrons kept asking about you. Everyone's been supportive."

"Yeah." The show of solidarity at the courthouse made her feel appreciated and awkward at the same time. It was what they did. She preferred not to be at the center of it. "Thank you so much. We better go in case Valerie needs to talk to us."

"I'll be here. I guess no walk in the park for us today. It's supposed to rain until the weekend."

"I don't think this little girl is much in the mood for anything today." Jordan leaned in to place a kiss on Meri's cheek.

"I get her," Ellie said. "But we have the weekend off, that's something."

"You want to come over on Sunday?" Pauline asked. "They said on the news the weather's going to get pretty bad, but I don't assume we'll get the brunt of it."

"We'll think about it. Let's just take it day by day."

❧

"You did great. She had nothing on you." Valerie Esposito handed Ellie a hot coffee, content with Ellie's testimony, and herself. She had called Ellie as a pre-emptive strike. She hadn't been on the case, and she shouldn't have gone into the room, but every word spoken during that tense exchange was further proof of the charges Valerie had filed.

Ellie realized her hands were trembling after being confronted with the recording once more, up to the moment Joy Anne spat at her, and Bethany entered the room.

"I sound like me in that footage," she said. "And it's what I would have told her anyway, what I thought someone needed to tell her...but I barely remember going inside. It's unreal."

"The most important thing is that you kept your cool, no matter how hard it was. She spat at you, for Christ's sake."

Jordan, standing in the corner, winced. She came over to Ellie and laid a hand on her shoulder. "Valerie is right. They thought they could use it against us, and it came back to bite them."

"I'm glad we're all on the same page here," Valerie said softly. "Now I trust you to bring it home."

Jordan's testimony, for maximum effect, would be closer to the end, before Joy Anne Deane's. No one could deny the facts after they had seen the video.

Ellie took another sip of her coffee, relishing the warmth, wondering if it would ever feel like enough, whatever sentence Joy Anne got in the end.

⁂

Joy Anne Deane was wearing a blouse and skirt, her hair down, no make-up. She was younger than the lawyer and looked the part. Would the jurors at some point feel sorry for her, thinking she might be intimidated by the many cops in the room? Jordan focused on Valerie standing in front of her, her own narrative, the truth. That had to be enough.

Of course, Deane's lawyer found something to challenge. Jordan knew why. She was working hard to sow doubt in the mind of the jurors that Joy Anne was fully responsible for her crime.

"We know that Joy Anne has for a long time been under the influence of the Prophets of Better Days, whose doctrine did include discrimination against alternative lifestyles."

"Alternative lifestyles? You mean—"

"I'm sorry, Detective. This is my question. Do you remember what exactly she said to you in the parking garage?"

"I do," Jordan said, calmly, though she felt disgusted by the lawyer trying to reframe Joy Anne's actions. "She said 'You took away my children.'"

"And were you directly responsible for her losing custody?"

"Directly, no. I suppose dismantling the Prophets was the beginning of the end, but I work in Homicide. I had nothing to do with the case that led to her loss of custody."

"Hm. Thank you for clarifying that. Did she say something else?"

"Something along the lines of 'Now you pay.' She stabbed me again, then she ran."

141

"She didn't mention Ariel, or your marriage to a woman, in that moment?"

"No." This wasn't good, Jordan could tell from Valerie's expression.

"Did she say that you being a cop had anything to do with her actions?"

"Not directly, but given where it happened, I think it's pretty clear..."

"Thank you, Detective, please just answer the question."

"I did. They answer is no."

It went on across the same lines. She was trying to steer the jurors away from the hate crime, and towards an insanity defense.

Jordan had faith in the expert witness Valerie would call, but she was tired. The end of this couldn't come soon enough—especially when she made the mistake looking over to Joy Anne Deane.

The woman smiled.

"Ms. Deane, did someone tell you to attack Detective Carpenter?"

"No." Her voice was almost a whisper. The judge instructed her to speak into the microphone. She cleared her throat and repeated, "No."

"Why did you do it?"

Her eyes filled with tears. "I sat home alone, without my children, every day. I miss them so much! I can't live without them. I wanted to die."

"But at some point, you made the decision to go after Detective Carpenter."

The defense lawyer looked like she wanted to object, but she stayed silent, on the edge of her seat.

"Because you remembered her."

"Objection!"

Before she could elaborate, A.D.A. Esposito pushed on. "You remembered that Detectives Carpenter and Harding were going to adopt Ariel Deane, and you objected to the idea."

"Objection! Your Honor, she's putting words into my client's mouth."

"Sustained. Counselor, please, ask a question."

"Of course. I apologize, Your Honor. Ms. Deane, please clarify for us—why Detective Carpenter? Was it because you objected to her family life?"

Joy Anne cast a quick look at her lawyer who nodded, before she answered.

"I had tried to call my children, but they wouldn't let me talk to them. I was...so desperate. I wanted to talk to someone, get help...everything else is a blur."

"You wanted to get help to communicate with your children, and you brought a knife?"

"Like I said, it's a blur. I might have picked it up at home. All I wanted was to see my little ones. I don't know what I said to her, I swear!" The lawyer looked satisfied with her answer. Valerie made a small pause, which Joy Anne used to correct the record. Her voice was firm when she spoke. "This is the truth. That doesn't mean I approve of their lifestyle or ripping children away from the only family they know and love. That is all. I thought it was important you knew that," she said directly to the jurors. "Our society is deteriorating, and this is all a part of it. We tried to be pure."

"Thank you, Ms. Deane." Valerie could barely keep the triumph out of her voice. Joy Anne's speech had made more than one juror's jaw drop.

# Chapter Twenty-Two

The guilty verdict blew up the Internet with opinions. Ready to go home and spend some time with her family away from the circus, Ellie made the mistake of doing more than a quick check on the phone. The majority of people discussing the news expressed relief that Joy Anne Deane would be held accountable, but the voices wanting to elevate her to martyrdom, were already coming out, to no surprise.

The door of the break room opened, and without looking up, Ellie reached for her coffee.

"Sometimes I hate people," she said, assuming that the person who walked in, could relate. "They were quick to forget that the Prophets abused women and children over decades. Now they want to throw money at her?"

"Go home. Put up your feet, take a moment to breathe," Derek advised.

"Yeah, I should," she acknowledged with a sigh. "Is Jordan waiting for me?"

"I think she's had enough of people congratulating her, so probably, yes."

Ellie cast another look at her screen, an opinion blog saying that putting Joy Anne behind bars might muddle the issues and keep other women from getting the help they needed.

She tossed her phone on the table hard enough to make Derek wince.

"This is all we ever wanted, help the women and children in that Goddamned place. No, they don't get it. She's a criminal. Muddle the issues? Doing anything but hold her accountable will muddle the issues."

Derek had apparently enough context to understand what she meant—or he'd read the same blog.

"I agree. And I can tell you everyone outside this door agrees as well. They married off fourteen-, fifteen-year-olds, and there was a graveyard on the compound. Don't get distracted."

"I won't. Thanks. I'll see you tomorrow."

Ellie picked up her phone and turned it off. She went in search of Jordan, finding her at her desk, Casey Lyons standing next to her.

"Go home, kids," Casey said. "It's a win."

"Sounds like a good plan. Jordan?"

"Yes, please."

<hr>

With Meri asleep, they decided to make it an early night, even though there were still things to address.

"We didn't really have much time to talk about this, but how do you feel now that the Boyd case is closed?" Ellie knew Jordan had been troubled by this outcome.

Jordan sighed. "We had no choice, but this doesn't feel right."

"You've had a lot on your plate." Ellie chose her words carefully. She knew they were the truth, yet she didn't want Jordan to take them the wrong way.

"You think I'm projecting."

"Are you?" Ellie asked softly.

"Maybe, maybe not, I'll have to let it go anyway. Jerry doesn't want to press charges. I can still put out the word, see if we're really dealing with something random here. I think I just hate the world a little."

Scooting closer, Ellie said, "I know what you mean. And I understand, but they won't win. We have to remind ourselves of that."

"That the pendulum will swing our way at some point—and then back again? I'll get over it. I have you, and Meri, and we have some great people in our lives. Not everyone is that lucky."

"But Boyd's death didn't have anything to do with bad luck. Perhaps it had nothing to do with the fact that he was gay. It's tragic, but it might be coincidence that those incidents happened the same night. We might never know. You still need time to heal. That doesn't mean you can't trust your instincts. She'll never have that much power."

"You're right. As always." Jordan's hand was gentle in her hair. "Thank you for putting up with all that. I swear at some point I'll stop adding more drama to our lives."

"You don't need to apologize. None of it was your fault."

Jordan didn't argue one way or another, but she tightened her arms around Ellie. For the moment, this was enough of an answer.

❦

Another morning began with rain and overcast skies, though Jordan was relieved to feel better than she had in weeks. Ellie had made breakfast and now sat at the table with Meri in her lap. Jordan hated the world a lot less this morning as she finished her coffee.

"Jack and Pauline are doing some shopping for the *SEVEN* today, so I thought I could join them and leave Meri with them afterwards," Ellie announced. "We should stock up for Nora too. Is there anything you want?"

"Nora? Oh, the storm. Why would we stock up? I thought we were going to order in?"

Ellie cast a doubtful look at her phone, where the weather app was open. "I'm not even sure they're going to deliver. According to the news, it's going to be wild out there."

"How wild? We don't get that kind of storm around here."

"Apparently now we do, thank you very much, climate change deniers. Perhaps it's not going to be so bad, but we should be prepared."

"Okay. The usual. Some pizza?"

"Sure. Power might be out though. Do we have everything we need for Meri?"

"I guess another pack of diapers couldn't hurt. Some bananas maybe? Otherwise, we'll be fine. Oh, wait. Flour. I feel like having some waffles for breakfast."

"Good idea. I feel bad saying that, but I'm almost glad I'm not in uniform anymore. It's going to be all hands on deck. Most people just want to help, but some can get nasty under circumstances like this."

Somewhat guiltily, Jordan realized that she hadn't paid much attention to anything outside of the immediate issue, Joy Anne Deane's trial and its outcome. That was how much power she'd given her.

"I'm glad, too. If it's selfish, so be it. Honestly, I wish we didn't have to go in at all today."

Ellie shrugged. "If we want to take the weekend off, we should. Don't worry. The worst of the storm is supposed to happen later tonight. We'll both be home by then."

"All right. I'd like to spend some more time with my two favorite people, but I guess work is calling. Literally," Jordan added when her own phone rang. "You two have fun. See you later."

After a quick kiss for each of them, she left, answering the phone as she walked outside.

"Carpenter."

"Hey, it's me," Derek said. "Jerry Morgan is here. He says he received some threats...and he wants to press charges now."

"I'll be right there." Trust her instincts, Ellie had said, and she was right. Oliver Boyd's death had been ruled a suicide, and they might not ever be able to prove otherwise. But there was a lot more to discover about what happened that night, and none of it had to do with paranoia on Jordan's part.

On the drive, she listened to the radio, everyone worked up about the upcoming, possibly record-breaking storm. Even with the continuous rain, it was hard to imagine a weather event like this, in this region and season. They expected some power outages and minor damages in the city, the possibility of flash flooding in some areas. Their friends and colleagues in uniform would have their hands full, no doubt about it.

At the station, she found Jerry Morgan with Derek at his desk.

"Hi," she said, shaking Morgan's hand before she took off her coat. "I'm glad you changed your mind. Can I ask what the reason was?"

He looked a lot better than the last time she'd seen him, though doubtful.

"I'm not sure if it's not too late?"

Jordan wasn't going to lie to him. "It would have been better to file the report right away, but we'll see what we can do. Another detective might want to talk to you. For now, we're okay to handle this." She was aware of the look Derek gave her, ignoring him for the moment.

"Good. I heard that Deane woman was found guilty."

Jordan only hoped he wouldn't say "congratulations." People meant well. It didn't feel right. She wanted her life back, a sense of safety. She might have made steps in the right direction, but Jordan felt far from victorious. Joy Anne going to prison was only a logical consequence of her actions. It wasn't enough for peace.

"When I heard that," Jerry continued, "I realized I might have a shot. Whether you catch him or not, it's going to be on the record. That I said something. I know you're a cop, but it can't have been easy for you, to sit in court and recount what happened."

*It wasn't fun. It wasn't the hardest part.* Jordan voiced none of her thoughts. Instead, she forced a smile.

"No, but I'm glad I did it. Like I said, someone else might take your case, but we will do whatever we can to find who attacked you. Has Detective Henderson already gone over everything with you?"

"We were just talking about the threats," Derek answered. "Emails, and a couple of notes in the mailbox."

"Yeah, I brought them. The emails are here on my phone." Morgan had already put them in a plastic bag.

"Did anyone else touch these?" Jordan asked.

"After I found them, only me."

Reading both of the notes, she felt a flash of nausea. Nothing new in the grand scheme of things, but still frustrating. People resisting change, others making excuses for them. Joy Anne and her crowd-funding campaign.

"This happened over what period of time?"

"The first email came...Wednesday. Since then, an email and a note every day."

"Someone has a lot of time on their hands," Derek remarked. There was a slight edge to his voice that told Jordan he felt the same way about the person behind those slurs. "Nevertheless," he continued, "We're going to get these to the lab. Maybe we're lucky and they'll find prints."

"Let's find out. Jerry, aside from the incident that night, have you had any concerning interactions with anyone lately? Someone who might do this?"

He shook his head. "The people I know either accept me, or they've made their peace. No one I can think of."

"Okay. We will let you know what we find out. In the meantime, be mindful of your surroundings."

Jerry shook his head with a bitter laugh. "Nothing new, is it? Just when you think we're past all that crap."

"We'll be in touch," Jordan said. "I promise. You still have my card?"

"Yeah. Thank you."

She got up to walk him out and tossed her coat over her chair as they passed by her own desk. This might have nothing to do with Boyd, but at least it was a step forward. It seemed like that was all they could do at this point, small steps.

# Chapter Twenty-Three

The rain was coming down harder when Ellie drove to the station. The highway was already blocked in some parts. She took the next exit for a different route. It came with a small detour. All things considered, she hoped she'd still save time.

She had to drive slower but was lucky to find the road mostly empty. Most of the time Ellie enjoyed driving in these more rural parts surrounding the city. All she wanted on this day was for it to end. She wasn't fooling herself—she and Jordan still had some talking to do, and the more time passed, the more both of them would be tempted to let it slide. She was happy Jordan was doing well, able to work again. The nightmares seemed to have abated, and Meri had overcome her fussy, restless phase. But Ellie knew Jordan was still struggling with the ending of the Boyd case.

Truth be told, she was struggling too, waiting for the other shoe to drop. It was an unfamiliar and uncomfortable feeling for Ellie. She wanted it gone. A quiet weekend might not do away with all of it, but it was a start.

After another mile, the road narrowed to a one-way street. That's when she saw the car stopped on the side, lights flashing.

A man was kicking his front tire before he leaned down for further examination. Ellie didn't blame him. Stepping outside for a minute or so would soak a person in this weather. She was likely about to find out because she couldn't pass him by without landing halfway in a ditch.

And perhaps that was the plan? She stopped, making sure she had cell phone reception, and exited her car, moving her hand closer to her gun. Too many stories existed about men faking an emergency like this.

"Sir, what's the problem?" She almost had to shout over the wind. At first, Ellie thought he didn't understand her, but then she heard. "Blew out my tire. Isn't that obvious?"

He straightened and faced her. Ellie relaxed her arm at her side, though part of her wished she'd turned her car around.

Cliff Waters, her former partner, groaned. "Of course. On this day of all days."

"Right. Great to see you, Cliff." She couldn't help it, even though sarcasm had never been the best defense with the man who had gone from being a nuisance to a complete disgrace. She was almost ready to walk away when she saw the passenger in his car.

The night shift would have to deal with the brunt of the storm, though reports of flooded basements in lower-located areas were already coming in.

"I'm really grateful for our twelfth-floor apartment right now," Derek remarked when they'd sat down for a quick lunch. "You're not going to have any trouble?"

"God, no. No more trouble. We didn't get any specific warnings for where we live. Ellie and I plan to hide away with the baby for the weekend."

"Good plan. Kate's sister wanted to visit this weekend, but she postponed."

"You are all starting to freak me out. I'm going to leave a bit earlier, I think. The lab's not going to have anything on Jerry's case today, and that paperwork can wait until Monday."

"If you're bored, I have some calls on my list you could make for me," Maria Doss, who had appeared behind her, remarked. "On second thought, I think I'll stay here and do them myself. It's just getting worse out there."

"Come on, that's a bit dramatic."

"You didn't wonder why it's so quiet around here? Everyone is out there."

Jordan had the terrifying vision of neither of them being able to go home to Meri tonight. Pauline would stay and take good care of her, but they needed to have this weekend as a family. Get their bearings after the past few months.

"I think I'm going to check what Ellie is up to," she announced.

***

"Detective...Harding, right? Nice to see you again, even if it's under the circumstances."

Joe Waters, Cliff's father, had helped Ellie out on a previous case. He had lowered the window and reached outside to shake her hand. This was better and worse at the same time. Waters senior had turned out to be a lot nicer than anyone had expected, given his son's behavior. She couldn't back out now.

"You too." She turned to her former colleague who was glaring at her like he had for most of the time they'd worked together. This was nothing new. "You need help with that tire?" she asked anyway.

"You can change a tire?" he asked with an incredulous laugh.

155

"Cliff, come on. That's beside the point now," his father said. "Because someone forgot the spare tire."

"I'm on my way to work, but I could give you a ride."

"I don't think—"

"That would be delightful," Joe Waters interrupted his son. "Thank you so much, Detective Harding. Ignore him. He hasn't had enough coffee today."

Ellie chose not to answer. While she liked the older Waters, she didn't have the same perspective. After all, Cliff Waters wasn't a wayward teenager. He had assaulted two of their colleagues. He still blamed Ellie, who had been a witness to one incident, for the consequences that had followed. But she couldn't leave the two of them in the worsening weather either.

"Okay, get in. We just have to back up a little."

Cliff Waters went into the front passenger seat without asking, leaving the backseat to his father. His father sat next to the baby seat.

Ellie saw Cliff's pensive look, though she hoped he wouldn't get too obnoxious in front of his father.

"We had lunch in town. Everyone is talking about the storm. If it's true what they say, we haven't seen anything like it in this area."

"That's not true," Cliff Waters muttered.

Ellie knew his stance on climate change. She wasn't going to walk into that discussion, now, or ever.

"Congratulations, by the way. How old is the baby?" Either Waters senior was completely unaware of the tension, or he enjoyed irritating his son even more. Ellie wasn't sure which one it was.

"Four months," she answered. Seeing the disdain in her former partner's expression, she barely refrained from the impulse to kick him out. Usually, she felt like she had to explain that Jordan had done the hardest part, but at the moment, she wanted to escape the subject matter. Discussing anything about her private life in front of Cliff seemed wrong. She knew he objected to her being able to marry and have a family. Her parents didn't live to see all the good she had in her life, but she knew they'd had a zero tolerance for bigotry, and they had instilled that in her too.

"Enjoy the time. They grow so fast."

And if she'd had a dime for everyone who ever told her that, she could have taken today and all days off. Suppressing a sigh, Ellie smiled and then turned back onto the highway.

"Are you crazy? We're going to be stuck for hours!" Cliff Waters snapped at her.

His father was silent, perhaps disturbed at the overly hostile tone.

"You already got stuck in the middle of nowhere, remember? I'm not going to take the risk. It's this, or you walk."

She was sure he was having a hard time holding in the slur he would have hurled at her, were they alone in the car. A smile tugged at the lips of Joe Waters.

❧

Jordan stepped into the elevator, more than ready to go home. For the sake of the people who had to work, including some of her colleagues, she hoped the storm wouldn't get too bad. She and Ellie, and everyone they knew, had stocked up in case of power outages or flooding. They were most likely going to be lucky, but these days, you never knew. At least Kathryn and Jim had finally moved out of the trailer and into a modest apartment.

The elevator came to a halt, and the doors opened with a soft sound, Bethany stepping inside. She was carrying an oversized bag and pulling a small suitcase.

"You're heading home?"

"Oh yes. I got a cab waiting for me, and I hope Nora isn't messing with traffic already. I need to make it onto that plane."

"Good luck," Jordan offered. "I didn't know you stayed in town this long."

"Well, it was for work...I did go home but came back for the trial. I wanted to see that woman go behind bars for a long time. Isn't it ironic how bigots have the power to bring us together?"

Jordan chose not to comment further on Bethany's collaboration with Valerie. Truth be told, she'd take any chance to avoid talking about Joy Anne Deane more than necessary. She was immensely grateful for friends who were professionals to the bone, eager to see justice work.

"Yeah, maybe." The elevator lurched, enough for Bethany's suitcase to fall over with a bang, and stopped. The number still said "4" but the doors didn't open.

"Oh, for Christ's sake, on this day of all days," Bethany muttered, while Jordan pressed the emergency button. She heard some static, but no one answered.

"Don't worry. It's a busy place. Someone will get us out of here in no time."

"Or they already went home for the weekend."

"And you always said I was the pessimist. Hey! Can you hear me?"

Bethany sighed. "You shouting isn't going to make them magically appear, you know."

"If you have a better idea, let me know." Jordan banged her fist against the door a few times. Feeling silly, she stopped. Bethany glanced at her watch.

"Damn. I'm sure someone has snatched my cab already." Checking her phone, she muttered another curse. "No reception. Of course."

Jordan checked her own, just to come up with the same result.

"I would drive you, but...hey, I'm sorry." Based on past experience, Jordan almost expected Bethany to blame the inconvenience on her. At least they were long past that. "If it makes you feel any better, I'm nowhere closer to getting home to my wife and child."

"Yeah. I'm sorry too. I just hoped I'd have a chance to see my girlfriend this weekend, but with my luck, they grounded the plane because of the storm."

"She's campaigning with her dad?" Bethany had been dating Debra Connelly, the daughter of a Democratic senator, for almost a year.

"Very visibly so. My parents still flinch every time the name Connelly is mentioned on TV."

"At least they're not going to disown you." Jordan knew it was a small comfort for her ex, but it was all she could offer. Mr. and Mrs. Roberts weren't going to change the habits, or the party affiliation, of a lifetime.

"Not yet. I'm not sure they'll come to the wedding either."

"Oh, are you...Congratulations."

"Just a figure of speech. I'm not sure either one of us is ready, especially with all that traveling going on."

"You have to make an effort to spend time together, no matter how crazy the job is."

Bethany shook her head, laughing wryly. "This is the twilight zone. I'm stuck in an elevator, getting relationship advice from Jordan Carpenter. No offense."

"Oh, I definitely take offense. That was mean."

"Yeah, it was. I'm sorry. I hate that now I won't be able to see Debra in weeks." She paused for a few seconds. "I don't regret coming back though. Esposito had a strong case, and I wanted to be there for the verdict."

"I'm so glad it's over."

Bethany's expression softened.

"I'm happy you're doing better. Working again. That must have been tough, coming here."

"I survived. But it was...tough." No point in lying to the shrink, especially when she couldn't go anywhere.

"I can imagine."

The lights flickered. Jordan welcomed a distraction, though not this one. "Oh no." She'd barely finished speaking when the emergency lights came on.

"Well, Ellie will at some point notice that you're late, right? It's a freaking police station, the elevator stops working, someone will realize there are people in here?"

"You're making good points. I think."

Jordan couldn't imagine that no one would think to check—then again, a lot of her colleagues had either gone home early or were out helping others. She and Bethany were safe if highly inconvenienced by the situation.

"I should. I make a living from that." Not that she needed to remind Jordan. "So, how's family life with the third party?"

"I doubt you're interested in that."

"You're still mad at me about the last time we talked? I'm sorry. I didn't mean you could never change your mind. For sure it stopped being my business a long time ago."

"I'm not mad. I just don't think...never mind." Jordan sat on the floor and leaned against the wall. Still no cell phone reception. She had to remind herself that this was nothing compared to the people who had to be out in this weather for whatever reason. She had survived much worse. None of these thoughts helped her mood. After a few seconds ticked by, Bethany sat down next to her but remained silent. It didn't take long for the situation to feel claustrophobic. They had made amends over the years, but there was still a lot of history between them. Not all of it good.

"It's been great," she said out loud. "There were moments when I thought I'd be bad at...all of it, and I still think that sometimes. But overall, I'm not doing so bad. I didn't turn into my mother."

"And, of course, Ellie." Bethany leaned against the wall. "Look, I meant what I told you the other time. There was a time when we were good together, but it didn't last. It turned into something like addiction, but we moved on. We're better now. I'm glad you're happy."

"Thanks. You too." Wasn't that the subject she kept circling around? What if it didn't last? Ellie had made it clear, she wasn't going anywhere. But some things were out of their control, like a criminal showing up in the parking garage with a knife. If she'd been a bit stronger, a bit more out of her mind...

"I almost didn't come back from it."

It had taken her some time to come to terms with her own mortality in a way she'd never had before, not even after the Darby case. In those days, Jordan had trouble believing anyone could truly need her. She'd been between relationships and homes, with a lot left to prove. Many things were different now. The idea that someone might be able to take her away from the life she'd built, from the people she loved, was terrifying her still.

"That's not surprising. You have to go back to where it happened every day. Did you take enough time?"

"Enough is a big word. I don't want to do anything else. I'm good at it."

"You will figure it out," Bethany said as the lights flickered. "If we ever make it out of here, that is."

# Chapter
# Twenty-Four

T ime was passing by, and Cliff Waters didn't stop complaining. They were stuck in traffic on the highway, but at the moment, Ellie didn't see any alternative.

"Look, it's not going faster. You are still free to walk the rest of the way."

"Really, Cliff, that's unnecessary. It was very nice of Detective Harding to take us."

"Thanks for the vote of confidence, Mr. Waters. I'm afraid that we'll be here for a while, but it will clear up eventually. There'll be a lot more branches blocking the smaller roads."

"Exactly. And you can call me Joe. We already worked together," he said with a wink, while his son rolled his eyes.

"We did. I'm Ellie."

"What the hell are you doing, Dad?"

"You're asking me that, really? I think we've all put up with your attitude for too long. And that's not even the worst of it, as we all know."

"This is not the time," Cliff, red-faced, muttered.

"Maybe it is, because you haven't listened to me."

Ellie wanted to be anywhere but in the car during this difficult father-son conversation. She got her wish when the car in front of her hit the brakes so abruptly she barely avoided hitting them.

⁂

"What are you doing?" Jordan asked incredulously when Bethany took out her laptop, opened a file and started to write.

"Well, it doesn't look like anyone's getting us out anytime soon. I might as well get some work done."

"I can't believe this. Hello?" Back on her feet, Jordan shouted to no one. "We're in here! Can you hear us?"

"Maybe they can and chose not to answer. Maybe this is all a psychological experiment. Or we time traveled."

"What did you smoke?"

Bethany looked up from her screen.

"I'm not going to dignify that with an answer, but you will have to get used to idea that we will spend some more time in here. You're disappointed, I am too. This is not how I envisioned my night either."

All of a sudden, the cabin lurched slightly, dropping maybe a couple of inches, startling them.

"All right," Bethany said as she put her notebook away. "I'm with you. This is no longer fun. And don't take this the wrong way, but I don't want to be buried with you. Not anymore."

Jordan raked both hands through her hair, more shaken than she wanted to admit to her ex, or herself. She was starting to feel nauseated, worry, hunger, it was hard to define. "Just stop."

⁂

Traffic had come to a complete halt. Ellie had gotten out of the car to see what happened a few vehicles in front of her, the wind whipping her hair into her face. A flatbed truck had lost its insufficiently secured load. Wood and metal had spilled out on the street, causing one driver to hit the guard rail as they tried to evade the mess. People were already standing around, filming with their phones.

Ellie held up her badge. "Has someone called an ambulance?" She pulled out her own cell phone when all she got in return were blank stares. Fortunately, there was reception now that they were out of the woods, literally, if not figuratively speaking.

"Over here!" The truck driver who had lost his cargo waved to her, and she stepped over bent metal and splintered wood to get to the car with its nose embedded in the guardrail. Inside, the driver, a woman in her forties, looked groggy and confused. Her airbag had opened.

"Ma'am, I'm with the police. An ambulance is on its way." It would get through eventually. The wind was howling now.

"My head hurts," she said. "I'm cold."

"Are you hurt anywhere else?"

"I don't think so."

That didn't sound too reassuring. Adrenaline often prevented people from feeling the pain of a traumatic injury right away...Ellie couldn't help flashing on the scene she had imagined over and over again ever since Lieutenant Carroll had called her into her office that day. She took a deep breath, willing away the nausea.

"I can't get out."

From what Ellie could see, the damaged dashboard had her boxed in, though she could still move her legs somewhat.

"I'll stay here with you," she promised and hurried around the car where she managed to open the door on the passenger side. "Help will be here soon. They'll get you out."

"I need to call someone. My daughter is still waiting at school. They wanted us to get them early because of Nora, but I couldn't get off work."

"I understand. I never made it to work." She kept talking to the woman, while casually checking her. To her relief, Ellie didn't find any serious injuries at first sight.

"I can't find my cell phone." The woman was close to tears.

"That's okay, I can call someone for you. What's your name?"

"Christine Ross."

"Okay, Ms. Ross, I'll try to reach somebody, but the lines might be overwhelmed. I'm sure there are other parents having this problem."

"I can't have this problem." She started to cry in earnest. "I'm in a custody battle."

"We'll figure it out," Ellie assured her. "Let me see what I can do."

To her surprise, she managed to get someone from the principal's office on the phone and handed it to Christine Ross. Ellie jumped when there was a knock on the window, and she turned to see a familiar face. Jill Allen, a local reporter, looked drenched, but that didn't seem to bother her.

"Hey. Jill. Now is not the time."

"I think it is. I'm afraid one of the people stuck in this mess is about to give birth."

Ellie felt the blood drain from her face. "An ambulance is on its way."

"They might not make it in time. It's the red Volvo."

"Okay. Could you stay with Ms. Ross here? I'll go."

For a moment she wished she had taken Jordan's advice. But she'd already backed out of a responsibility, if for a good reason. Ellie prayed that the baby could wait a little bit longer.

"Thank you! You're an angel."

Bethany did everything but wink at the young elevator technician who blushed at her words.

"Just doing my job," she said. "I'm sorry this took a while."

"Better late than never. Now, I can go spend the night at the airport—if I get there, that is."

Jordan's first call was to Pauline.

"Somehow, I imagined you would have quite the day. Jack closed the bar today, and we stayed here with Meri. Ellie called earlier too. I think she'll be home soon."

"She isn't home yet?"

Jordan cast a look at Bethany who stood leaning against the wall with her suitcase next to her, looking uncharacteristically lost. She suppressed a sigh. No matter how much distance they had gained from each other, no matter how thankful they both were for the opportunities they'd been able to pursue without one another...There was still a small part of her feeling like she owed her. Maybe it was just what a friend would do. Maybe it would make this day even more awkward.

"Nothing bad. She's stuck in traffic."

"Okay. Can you hang on a second?"

She covered the microphone with her hand. "If you want, you can stay with us for the night and go to the airport tomorrow?"

Jordan almost hoped that Bethany would come back with a sarcastic return, but the instant relief in her expression told her that wasn't likely.

"Really?"

"Yes, really. Just let me finish..." She pointed to her phone.

"Sure. Thank you so much."

"It's no problem." To Pauline, she said, "I have Bethany here. She missed her flight, so she's going to stay with us."

"Of course. How is she?"

Jordan couldn't find any clue from Pauline's tone as to how she received that news. "She's fine. We just got stuck in the elevator at the station, but we'll come home as soon as possible."

"Great. I'm sure you'll be hungry."

# Chapter Twenty-Five

"You're here." Ellie, with Meri in her arms, leaned in to kiss her, pointedly ignoring whatever might be awkward about the situation. "You wouldn't believe what happened on the way to work. In fact, I never made it there. Hi, Bethany."

Her gaze became a bit pensive at the sight of the suitcase. Jordan hastened to explain. "Bethany missed her flight, and they were canceled anyway, so I thought..."

"Oh, yes, sure, it's fine. I brought a guest for dinner, too. We almost delivered a baby...I'm happy to say the ambulance got through first, but it was close."

Ellie was dressed in a T-shirt and sweats. So, she had time to take a shower after what seemed like a turbulent day.

"Thank God there were only minor accidents. You're right on time for dinner."

"Thank you so much for having me."

Jordan wished she could have a moment with Ellie and Meri, but then again, she was hungry.

"Something smells great," she said. "Who's your guest?"

In the living room, she recognized Jill Allen and went to greet her. This day was full of surprises. Jack and Pauline shook hands with Bethany, the interaction between them polite as it had always been. Jordan was aware of Ellie watching the exchange with curiosity.

Finally, they could all sit down to eat. Jordan realized with irritation how exhausted she was. She had no good reason, did she? It wasn't like she'd had a hard day at work, and she'd spend a few hours of it stuck in the elevator. Not taking care of their daughter, like Ellie had this morning. Not serving and protecting, like Ellie had done for the rest of the day.

"The woman was so lucky," she said. "A few inches more, and her legs might have been crushed. Some of the back roads are still impassible, but the highway was okay when we left."

"Do you miss being out there every day?" Jill Allen asked.

"I didn't think I would, but it was...interesting. That was a big part of my life."

"But there's something to be said about a warm, dry office and a bigger paycheck," Bethany remarked.

"No kidding. So, you were on your way to DC?"

"Yes, but I guess I'll change my itinerary. No one will be waiting for me there. I might just go home tomorrow."

The conversation moved on to various subjects not Nora-related.

"Thank you for helping out today. I think it's bedtime for at least one of us." Jordan had meant those words for her parents only, but as she got up to take Meri out of her seat, she was aware of Ellie's concerned gaze. Ellie half rose, but she stopped her. "It's okay. I can take her."

One of the best things of their relationship was that they didn't always need so many words—Ellie seemed to understand without any further prompting that Jordan needed her to trust her. Upstairs, alone with Meri, Jordan sighed in relief.

"And how was your day?" she asked. Judging from the sounds and happy wriggling, she'd had a good one, unlike most of the city's population. Not that Jordan had a bad day, because she of all people should know the difference. She and Ellie had made it home safely, and all of their friends and family were accounted for. If everything was all right, why did she feel like breaking down? She'd done the work, confronted and exorcized her demons. No more.

There couldn't be more. Not when she still had to say good-bye to their guests and had come up with the ridiculous idea of harboring Bethany for the night.

Not tonight. Her reaction had spooked her, though she felt a bit calmer when Meri was asleep in her bed. Jordan went back downstairs.

Jill Allen was just about to leave. Jack and Pauline got up as well.

"One day we're going to cook you dinner, and you don't have to babysit first," Jordan promised as they hugged.

"But we love to do it," Pauline protested. "Not to say I won't let you cook when you have the time."

"We must do it soon." Ellie was still hyped up on the events of the day. When Jack, Pauline and Jill had left, she was quick to fill the ensuing silence. "Okay. What about a nightcap? Bethany?"

"Oh, I don't know about that. You must be pretty exhausted, and I need to get to the airport early."

"Just one glass," Ellie insisted. "I think we could all use some unwinding. And you must tell me about the elevator situation. Today of all days."

"Yeah. I think we could have been more useful elsewhere."

Bethany seemed unburdened by those thoughts. "Well, from the looks of it the folks who were out there got it under control. Thanks, Ellie. I'll have one glass."

Jordan wondered when the world had come to feel this absurd.

It wasn't just one glass. After a considerable period of abstinence, while trying to get pregnant, being pregnant, and afterwards, Jordan felt like a teenage girl on her first binge. While Ellie was asleep, she stole out of bed, restless and slightly nauseated.

Why?

She stared at her tired reflection in the bathroom mirror, trying to find any answer. Joy Anne Deane was found guilty, as it should be. She was back at work, and Ellie was back with the team after her stint in the task force.

They had a happy, healthy baby and the support of family and friends.

"Pathetic," she mumbled. She'd done a pretty good job of keeping a façade in the past few weeks, but she could see the cracks appear. Most things in their lives were back to normal. She wasn't. The problem wasn't that she didn't want to talk to Ellie.

She didn't know what to say. All she could do was carry on and hope that at some point that hollow cold feeling would go away.

That moment seemed unattainable.

Fortunately, Bethany didn't have any intention of prolonging her stay more than necessary. Ellie was happy to provide her with a quick breakfast and see her out after Meri's needs were taken care of. Jordan was still asleep, and Ellie had seen no need to wake her.

"Say goodbye for me," Bethany advised. "And thank you, this was really kind of you."

"No problem. Have a good trip."

She went back into the kitchen and poured herself another coffee. Meri had been a little cranky and, from the looks of it, in need of sleeping in. A nap would take care of that. Ellie was more worried about Jordan. She didn't want to be worried, leave her space to deal with everything at her own pace, but she couldn't help wondering if she'd already overstepped, pushed too hard. Having a plan was something Ellie needed, because it always made her feel better, with challenges big and small.

Perhaps they could still have the quiet weekend they'd been hoping for and try to find some answers to these questions. She wasn't sure what to think, but something didn't feel right.

Her mind wandered back to the day she'd confronted Joy Anne Deane in the interrogation room. Ellie knew that she didn't regret anything. She'd do it all over again, tell the truth to her, because it needed to be said, as often as possible.

"You did everything. Again."

She turned to Jordan who had just come downstairs.

"Ulterior motives. It worked. Bethany was grateful for the breakfast, and she left early."

"About that, I'm sorry. I didn't have time to warn you."

"It's fine. I think her weekend plans took a bigger hit. Are you hungry?"

Jordan stepped closer, hesitant, but she sat down. "I guess."

Ellie got up to pour her some coffee.

"Thanks." Jordan picked up her cup and took a sip before she set it aside, pressing her hands against her face. Ellie was on her feet again in a second.

"I'm so sorry." To her relief, Jordan let herself be drawn into a gentle embrace. Ellie had to fight the impulse to bring out all the questions, what's wrong, how can I fix it, reminding herself that Jordan would tell her when she was ready.

"It's not you. You have nothing to be sorry for."

"Neither do you."

Ellie held on, because it felt like the right thing to do. Eventually, they would need to come up with a plan, together. Someone to talk to who didn't have a say in their professional future. She was going to raise the subject sometime this weekend, perhaps even today, but not now. There was nothing she could do right now but hold on.

She might have been wrong on Oliver Boyd. Unless a miracle happened, something they would need to break the case wide open, she'd have to live with it—this realization, and others. But there was much more to grieve for, and eventually, Jordan would tell Ellie how grateful she was to her for providing a safe space to let her do it. A sense of security. A sense of invincibility. She could do the job, do what was expected of her every day, but perhaps nothing would ever be the same. And maybe that wouldn't be a bad thing somewhere along the line.

# About the Author

B arbara Winkes writes sapphic crime drama and Christ-mas romance. She loves writing characters who get the job done, whether it's stopping a predator or saving cherished traditions—while still making time for love. She lives with her wife in Quebec City.

barbarawinkes.com

# Also by Barbara Winkes

**Luce Allen Mysteries**
*In Harm's Way*
*Under Pressure*

**The Crossing Lines Trilogy**
*Undercover*
*Redemption*
*Vengeance*

**The Connected Series**
*Promised to the Queen*
*Drawn to the Enemy*
*Tempted by the Protector*
*Saved by the Heiress*

**Carpenter/Harding**
*Indiscretions*
*Insinuations*
*Incisions*
*Intrusions*

*Initiations*
*Intentions*
*Infatuations*
*Impressions*
*Implications*
*Infractions*
*Incidents*
*Illusions*

**Kelli & Merin Romantic Suspense**
*Thunder*
*Rain*

***Lord and Burton***
*Clean Slate*

**Standalone**
*The Amnesia Project*